WELCOME TO THE GRAVEYARD

and Other Tales

A Collection by

Mark Allan Gunnells

Evil Jester Press

Welcome to the Graveyard and Other Tales
Copyright © 2014 by Mark Allan Gunnells

Evil Jester Press
Ridge, NY

First Edition: October 2014

ISBN: 978-0692303733

Printed in the United States and the United Kingdom

To my mother. You always worked so hard to provide a decent life for me, and I'm eternally grateful for that. Love you, Mama.

Introduction

by John R. Little

I've been writing horror and dark fantasy stories now for more than forty years. That seems impossible but it's true. Somehow the years drift by. Everyone faces the same path in some ways, and we all try to enjoy life as much as possible in the time we have.

During those forty years, I've also *read* horror, a ridiculous amount...I have no clue how many short stories in that time, but the number would certainly be in the high thousands. For many years, short stories were all that I read because that was what I wrote, and I knew the best way to improve your writing is to read the kinds of material you want to write.

So I did. I read all the short stories I could find by Stephen King, of course, but also Richard Matheson, Bentley Little, Gary A. Braunbeck, Richard Laymon, Rod Serling, Harlan Ellison, Rick Hautala, Shirley Jackson, and...well, you get the idea. I read every anthology and magazine I could find.

And what happened? Well, my writing did improve. No question. But there was an unexpected consequence of reading all those stories: I found myself not enjoying them as much now. Much of the short fiction I read has already been done by somebody else (usually better), the surprise ending aren't surprising at all, and lots of time I end a story wondering why I bothered.

So, when I read a collection where I feel that old sense of magic and enthusiasm I once felt, I know it's something very special. That is exactly what happened when I read Mark Allan Gunnell's new book, *Welcome to the Graveyard*.

My first introduction to Mark's writing was in his equally fine book, *Tales From the Midnight Shift*, which was published a few years back. I ordered that book just to say I'd tried it. It took only two stories for me to realize I was in the hands of a very special writer.

The stories you have in this book show a wide range. Some are very short, almost vignettes, some longer. Some are supernatural and some are based in our reality. Some have surprises while others lead us through an expected series of events. No matter what the differences among them, though, they all have one thing in common: the wonderfully fresh narrative voice that Gunnells gives us. His voice is unique and easy to tell. I have no doubt I could recognize a story of his in a pile of anonymous stories. He uses a minimum of wording, simplicity, average recognizable characters we get to know with a minimum of actual description, and we get carried away in the story immediately.

Some of these stories will stay with me forever. Each of us will have our own favorites, of course, but mine include "What's Done's Done," "What Little Boys are Made Of," and "Sunday Bath." I liked all these for different reasons, but they all had an impact on me.

Then there is the most memorable story of the bunch, a story that kicked me in the teeth and shook me for days. That, my friends, is the mark of a true writer. And, no, I'm not going to tell you what story I'm talking about. You have to find it yourself and see if you have the same reaction.

I envy people who have not yet read Mark Allan Gunnells, for they have a real treat ahead of them, and this book is the perfect place to start.

Enjoy!

Table of Contents

One day I was driving to work listening to a favorite song when I had a tire blow out. Nothing too serious, but a few weeks later I was driving along when that same song came on the radio, and I immediately tensed up, now associating that song with bad luck. I told myself I was being silly, that a certain song can't cause bad luck...and instantly the spark of the story was born. This story was originally published as a digital short with Darkside Digital in 2010.

Dancing in the Dark

"Can I look through your CDs?"

Breck glanced over from where he was hanging his shirts in the closet. Hayden was crouched over a cardboard box on which "CDs/DVDs" had been written in black magic marker. "Um, sure, knock yourself out."

Hayden folded back the flaps and started rummaging through the cases inside the box, twitching his nose like a rabbit to keep his glasses from sliding off. Breck shook his head and turned back to the task at hand.

The mundane job of stowing his clothes gave Breck an odd thrill in a way it never had before, but everything was different now. He was beyond excited to be starting college, away from home for the first time in his life and out from under his parents' thumb. Not complete freedom, life in the dorm still came with rules and the watchful eye of the R.A., but it was a definite first step toward full adulthood. He was going to have a blast this semester, he just knew it.

The only thing he was unsure of was the roommate he'd been stuck with. Hayden seemed a bit on the dorky side, bookish and withdrawn. They'd been in the room for a couple of hours, and Hayden had barely spoken, answering Breck's questions with caveman grunts. He'd shown no inclination to find out anything about Breck, at least not until the sudden interest in his CD collection. Breck was afraid he was rooming with a real buzz-kill. Then again, it was only the first day. Maybe Hayden would loosen up given time.

Breck was just placing the last of his sweaters on the small shelf at the top of the closet when he heard Hayden gasp, "Oh sweet Jesus, no."

"What's wrong?" Breck asked, turning toward his roommate.

Hayden was kneeling on the floor, staring down at a CD case in his hands with such abject horror and disgust that you'd think he was holding a flaming turd. "I was hoping you didn't have it. I mean, the chances were slim you would have it. And yet here it is, like the universe is just playing some fucked-up joke on me or something."

Breck frowned. "You got a problem with my musical taste?"

In answer, Hayden held the CD out toward him, pinching it from the very edge with just the tips of his fingers as if even touching it was repulsive. Breck saw that it was a copy of Bruce Springsteen's old album *Born in the U.S.A.*

"I didn't even realize I'd brought that along. My Dad gave it to me a couple of years ago when he was trying to get me to appreciate classic rock."

"Get rid of it," Hayden said in a strained voice.

"What?"

"Please, just get rid of it. I don't want it in the room."

Breck laughed uncertainly. "Not a Boss fan, I take it?"

Hayden tossed the CD away from him. It landed on the floor and skidded to Breck's feet. "I can't have it in this room."

"I don't get it." Breck picked up the CD and stared down at the cover, Springsteen's ass and that red bandanna. "I mean, it isn't really my kind of music, but the album's not that bad."

"It's not the whole album, just one song."

"Which one?"

"'Dancing in the Dark,'" Hayden said, spitting out the words as if they tasted foul in his mouth. His breath was coming in quick, shallow pants; it seemed as if he were on the verge of hyperventilating.

"I'm missing something here. What is it about that particular song that's got you spazing out?"

Hayden shifted position, sitting directly on the floor with his knees drawn up to his chest. His eyes were wide behind his glasses, and he looked very much like a frightened child who believed something nasty and vicious lived in his closet. "If I tell you something, do you promise not to think I'm crazy?"

"Dude, I already sort of think you're crazy."

Hayden nodded, grimaced, chewed on his bottom lip, then said, "That song's bad luck."

"What do you mean, *bad luck*?"

"Well, not for everybody. Just me. Whenever that song is played in my presence, horrible things happen."

"You're shitting me, right?"

Hayden didn't answer but looked both miserable and ashamed.

"What kind of horrible things?" Breck asked.

"Well, the first time was when I was about seven. I was in the car with my mother, she was bringing me home from school. The song came on the radio, and then BAM! A pick-up ran a red light and slammed into our car. My mom was killed instantly, I had a fractured skull and was in a coma for over a week."

"Jesus, man, that is horrible, but you seriously think it was because of the song?"

"Not at first, but when I was twelve I was playing at a friend's house. His father was watching VH1 and the video for the song came on, you know with that chick from *Friends* in it before the boob job. I tripped and fell down the basement steps, broke my arm in three places, busted out two teeth. When I was fifteen, I was at a school dance and they had mixed in some oldies with the current hits. They played that song, and suddenly I was in the most intense pain of my life. Turns out my appendix ruptured, had to have emergency surgery, I almost died. Then at seventeen, I was at a karaoke night at this teen club in my hometown, someone got up on stage and started singing that song. There was an electrical fire and…" Here Hayden paused and lifted his shirt, revealing the skin on the right side of his torso. It was pink and raised, rough-looking like scales. "From my nipple to mid-thigh on this side of my body. So now I do everything within my power to avoid having that song played in my presence. It's a matter of survival."

Silence followed, stretching out for several minutes. Breck wasn't sure what to say. Finally he cleared his throat and asked, "So you think, what? That Springsteen is out to get you or something?"

Hayden stood up, his posture rigid, his eyes cast downward. "I don't expect you to believe me, just...please get rid of that album."

Breck opened the case and popped the disc out. Its silvery surface reflected the overhead light, creating a rainbow pattern on the wall. "I admit, it's a freaky coincidence all that stuff happening to you while 'Dancing in the Dark' was playing, but it's just music. Music can't be good or bad luck. Maybe if we played it now, you'd see—"

"NO!" Suddenly Hayden was across the room, clawing and scratching at Breck, trying to get a hold of the CD.

Breck shoved his roommate hard in the chest, sending him to the floor. "Dude, you need to chill the fuck out. What are you, some kind of schizo?"

Hayden got on his knees, and there were tears streaming from his eyes now. "Please, I'm pleading with you. I'll do anything, just don't play that song."

Breck looked down at his roommate as if he were an alien. This guy was totally serious about this, he really thought the Springsteen song had the power to hurt him. Holding up his hands as if in surrender, Breck said, "Okay, I give. Like I said, it's not my kind of music anyway. See, I'm throwing it away right now."

Breck tossed the CD into the wastebasket by the desk on his side of the room. Hayden remained on his knees for a few seconds then scuttled over to the wastebasket, plucked the CD from it, snapped it into two pieces and let them fall back into the can. "Just to be on the safe side."

"Man, maybe you should see one of the campus counselors."

"Maybe," Hayden said, getting to his feet and wiping his eyes with the backs of his hands. He seemed to regain control of himself, as if the madness had passed now that the offending CD was destroyed, and he walked back over to his side of the room without another word, took a large framed poster of James Dean and placed it over his bed.

Great, Breck thought. *My roommate's crazy and a queer.*

a month later…

It was almost six in the evening, and Breck was hanging out in his room with his buddies Rick and Carlos. The two tennis players were stretched out on either end of Breck's bed, and Breck had turned the chair from his desk around and was sitting there, arms propped on the chair back. They were all drinking beers Rick's older brother had scored for them and passing around a joint.

"Man, too bad you guys aren't in my English Comp class," Carlos said, taking a hit. "Dr. Francesca was wearing the shortest leather skirt this morning, and she propped herself right up on the table up front. I bet the people in the first row got quite a peep show."

Rick's face contorted and he started making gagging sounds. "Dude, she's like a hundred and fifty."

"So what? Snatch is snatch."

"No, there is such a thing as good snatch and bad snatch," Breck said, taking the joint. Before starting college, he'd never even smoked a regular cigarette, but Rick and Carlos had introduced him to the wonders of marijuana. He didn't think he'd want to try any harder drugs, but he certainly enjoyed the pleasant disconnect he got from pot, the feeling that everything was all right, and if it wasn't...well, he just didn't give a fuck.

Carlos got up from the bed and started pacing. Pot seemed to make him kind of hyper. "So you guys are telling me you wouldn't have a go at Dr. Francesca if the opportunity presented itself?"

More gagging from Rick. "That would be like trying to fuck my Grandma."

"I thought all you southern boys already did that," Breck said with a high-pitched giggle.

Rick ignored him. "And you know her pussy's got to be all dried up and crusty and shit. Probably scrape the skin off your schlong just going in."

"Hey, I'm not saying she'd be my first choice, just that it's doable. If I had my pick of the litter, I'd go for that young art professor. What's her name?"

"Dr. Higgins," Rick said, inhaling, holding it, and letting the smoke leak out of his mouth toward the ceiling.

Breck couldn't seem to stop giggling. "Dr. Big Tits is more like it."

"I got one look at her during freshman orientation, I won't lie, I thought about switching majors."

"I tell you, I wouldn't mind —"

All three guys got instantly quiet and went rigid as the dorm room door swung open. Carlos, who was holding, tried to hide the joint behind his back but just ended up burning his fingers and dropping the blunt on the bed, burning a small hole in the coverlet.

Hayden walked into the room with his arms full of books, kicking the door shut with a foot. He paused and stared at the trio, who looked as if they'd just been caught gang-banging the preacher's daughter on the church altar.

"Oh, it's just you," Breck said with a sigh of relief, taking another swig of his beer. "I thought you had work study until eight."

"Not on Wednesdays, I've been at the library researching my World Civ paper." Hayden hurried to his side of the room, letting the mountain of books tumble onto his bed. He glanced back at the others, watching them drink and pass around the joint. "You know, you guys shouldn't be doing that."

Carlos laughed. "Man, if we didn't do any the stuff we shouldn't be doing, we'd never have any fucking fun."

"I'm serious, you guys could get into a lot of trouble. Normally I wouldn't care, but this is my room too, and you could get me into trouble by having your little booze and dope party here."

Breck rolled his eyes and rested his forehead on his hands. "Dude, lighten up, why don't you?"

"Here, have a toke," Rick said, holding out the joint.

"I'll pass. I'd rather keep all my brain cells, thank you."

Rick turned to Breck. "How do you live with this pansy-ass dickhead?"

"It's not easy, believe me."

Hayden stood by his bed, arms folded tightly across his chest. "Look, I hate to be this way, but I'm not going to risk getting kicked out of school for you guys. If you don't get that stuff out of my room right now, I'll have no choice but to go get Keith."

Keith Nyberg was the R.A. for their floor, and Breck had already had a few run-ins with him. Some Resident Advisors were known to be lenient and let certain violations slide; Nyberg was not one of them.

"Jesus, *Gay*den," Breck said, his roommate causing him to lose the peaceful buzz he'd had going, "now you're a tattle-tell on top of everything else?"

"Call me all the names you want, but you guys aren't just breaking school rules, you're breaking the law."

Rick took one final hit then licked his index finger and thumb and put out the joint, stowing it in his shirt pocket. "Fine, we'll go. My brother should be home from work soon; he'll probably let us party in his basement."

They all finished their beers and tossed the cans in the wastebasket. Rick stowed the rest away in his backpack. Hayden turned away from them, gathering up a few of the books he'd gotten from the library and taking them over to his desk.

Rick and Carlos headed out of the room, but Breck hesitated in the doorway, looking back at his roommate. Unable to help himself, he sang softly, "Even if we're just dancing in the dark..."

Then Breck walked out, slamming the door behind him, causing a heavy globe-shaped paperweight to fall off Hayden's desk and smash onto his foot.

two weeks later...

Breck and Rick were sitting on the low brick wall that circled the fountain out front of the administration building when Carlos came running up to them, red-faced and out of breath. "Did you guys hear?"

"Let me guess," Rick said. "You finally fucked Dr. Francesca and she crumbled to dust beneath you?"

Breck and Rick laughed, but Carlos did not join in. "Dudes, they searched my room for drugs."

This caused the laughter to dry up right fast. "Did they find your stash of weed?" Rick asked, his serious expression that of a parent asking if their missing child had been found.

"No way, man. Not even the people who built the dorm would be able to find my super secret hiding place."

Breck put a hand to his chest and let out a relieved sigh. "You had me scared there for a minute."

"You guys are missing the point here. They didn't search anyone else's room that I know of. Somebody must have tipped off Housing that I was carrying."

Breck and Rick exchanged a glance and spoke at the same time, the same word. "Hayden."

"That's it, that little fucker's getting his ass kicked all the way to Myrtle Beach and back," Rick said, jumping to his feet. "Somebody call for an ambulance, because he's going to need one when I'm through with him."

Breck reached out and grabbed his buddy's arm. "Dude, chill for a minute."

"Don't tell me to chill," Rick said, jerking his arm back. "That douche is trying to get us kicked out of school, he needs to be taught a lesson."

"Yeah, but if you go beat the shit out of him, you'll get kicked out for sure."

This seemed to calm Rick a little, and he sat back down. "Well, we have to do *something*. We can't just let him get away with it."

"Maybe we could plant some weed on him," Carlos suggested. "Turnabout's fair play and all that."

Breck thought it over for a minute then shook his head. "I don't know. If he did just report us for drugs, then we turn right around and report him...might seem suspicious."

"We could call it in whatchacallit...anonymously."

"Yeah, but it still might look fishy," Rick said. "Could blow up in our faces."

"What then?"

Rick seemed to give it some serious thought. "We can't hurt him physically, so we need something that'll really fuck with his head. You live with the guy, Breck. Any suggestions? Like is he afraid of heights or spiders, anything like that?"

Breck was silent for a moment. He of course knew the prefect Achilles' heel, but did he really want to tell his buddies about Hayden's bizarre phobia? It seemed an awfully low blow, to exploit something like that. Rick and Carlos were still staring at him, waiting, and he thought about what would have happened if Carlos's weed had been found.

"Okay," Breck said after taking a deep breath. "I think I have an idea."

the next day…

It was 8:30 at night when Hayden walked into the room. It was dark, and he reached for the light switch, but then Rick grabbed him from behind, clamping a hand over his mouth before he could scream. Hayden kicked out with his legs, but Carlos grabbed those, and the two tennis players carried Hayden over to his bed and pinned him there, Rick's hand still over his mouth.

Breck was hanging back, just watching it all. He felt maybe they were going too far. Sure, his roommate was a royal pain in the ass but this might be a bit much.

"Come on," Rick hissed. "The fucker's trying to bite me."

Breck hurried forward, carrying a pair of socks rolled up into a little ball and some duct tape. Rick removed his hand, and when Hayden opened his mouth to scream, Breck crammed the socks in the opening. This was covered with several strips of duct tape.

Carlos, who had been holding down Hayden's legs, motioned for Breck to take over while he dug something out of a paper sack. Even in the darkness, alleviated only by a small desk lap on Breck's side of the room, the items were recognizable as two pairs of fuzzy pink handcuffs.

"Where the fuck did you get those?" Rick asked with a laugh.

"That sex shop over in Spartanburg."

They used the cuffs to affix each wrist to the headboard. That just left Hayden's legs, which Rick took care of with some bungee cord. Their work done, the three friends stood back and stared down at Hayden, whose struggles were futile, whose screams were muffled by the gag and tape.

"I bet the little faggot likes being all trussed up like this," Carlos said. "Probably turns him on. Bet he's got a woody."

Rick shoved Carlos toward the bed. "Why don't you check and see?"

"Very funny."

Rick walked over to the bed himself and bent at the waist until his face was right in front of Hayden's, their noses almost touching. "We're going to leave you alone for a couple of hours to think about what you did. But don't worry, we'll leave you some tunes to keep you company."

Carlos walked over to Hayden's desk and picked up an object and held it out for Hayden to see. "It's my iPod. I have it set to play the same song over and over. Can you guess which one?"

Hayden suddenly got very still, and his eyes met his roommate's and held them. Breck could see pleading in those eyes, betrayal, and more than a touch of soul-numbing fear. Breck just turned away.

Carlos placed the iPod in a docking station with speakers, fiddled with it until the opening strains of "Dancing in the Dark" filled the room. He turned up the volume.

Hayden began going wild on the bed, bucking and jerking at his restraints, gnawing at his gag to the point Breck was afraid he'd swallow it. Breck was reminded of a documentary on demon possession he'd watched last month while stoned.

"Let's go," Rick said, leading his friends out of the room. Breck looked back at his roommate one final time and felt bad…but not bad enough that he didn't close and lock the door.

one hour later…

They were in the Student Center, Rick and Carlos shooting a game of pool while Breck sat on a stool nearby looking miserable.

"Jesus, what's wrong with you?" Rick said. "You look like somebody just dug up your Grandma and skull-fucked her corpse."

"I don't know, it's just that…we could still get into a lot of trouble for this."

"For what? What's Hayden going to say, that we forced him to listen to a song?"

"Well, we did tie him up."

"His word against ours," Carlos said, missing an easy shot and cursing.

Rick nodded. "I didn't put the cuffs on tight enough to leave any marks, so if he tries to make trouble, we'll just deny everything. Shouldn't be a problem as long as we all keep our fucking mouths shut."

"Yeah, I guess," Breck said, chewing on his bottom lip.

"And remember, he brought this on himself," Carlos said. "He should have never gotten my room searched."

A girl Breck recognized from his Psych 101 class was walking by the pool table, and she suddenly stopped and turned toward Carlos. "You too?"

"Me too what?"

"You had your room searched too? They did mine just today."

The three friends all looked at each other then back at the girl. Rick was the first to speak. "They searched your room?"

"Yeah, that's what I just said."

"Who ratted you out?" Carlos asked.

The girl frowned. "What are you talking about? The administration is trying to crack down on drug use on campus, so they're randomly selecting students' rooms to search. Haven't you noticed the announcements they put up all over campus?"

"Oh fuck," Breck said. "That means Hayden might not have done it after all."

Rick laughed. "Oops."

"Dude, it's not funny. We might be getting back at him for something he didn't even do."

"He's still a prick," Rick said with a shrug.

"Come on, we need to go let him loose right now and apologize."

Rick exhaled forcefully. "I guess you're right. Carlos, give him the keys to the cuffs."

"You're not coming with me?"

"Me and Carlos have a game to finish. Send Gayden our regrets."

Breck took the handcuff keys and hurried out of the Student Center, practically sprinting back to his dorm. As he was rushing down the hall toward his room, he passed Preston Donaldson from two doors down who said, "Hey, is your weirdo roommate actually getting some?"

"What?"

"Sounds like his headboard is banging against the wall. He's either getting some or he's a lot more aggressive with his wanking than I am."

Without responding, Breck took off toward his room again. Now he could hear it; underneath the sound of the Springsteen song, the sound of the headboard slamming against the wall. Apparently Hayden was trying so desperately to get free that he was moving the whole bed.

Breck fumbled his keycard from his wallet and was just unlocking the door when he heard a thud and the distinctive sound of glass shattering. Breck burst into the room, flipped on the light...

...and came to an immediately stop.

The bed was no longer slamming against the wall, because Hayden was no longer struggling. In fact, he wasn't moving at all. Of course, Breck couldn't see the upper half of his roommate's body, only his legs. It took Breck a moment to recognize what it was lying on top of Hayden.

The framed James Dean poster. Apparently the vibrations from the bed ramming the wall had knocked it loose and it fell on top of Hayden, the glass front shattering. Breck hurried to the bed, knocking the poster aside, and what he saw caused him to bend over and vomit on his shoes.

A large, jagged shard of glass had lodged itself in Hayden's throat, just below the Adam's apple. Blood bubbled up from the wound like a geyser, soaking the front of Hayden's shirt and his bedspread. His eyes, wide with terror, stared up at the ceiling, glassy and empty.

As Breck fumbled his cell from his pocket to call for help, he heard the Boss growling the chorus from the iPod.

"Can't start a fire, can't start a fire without a spark…this gun's for hire, even if we're just dancing in the dark…"

This story came from my musing on music, on how singing and songwriting are two different talents. And songwriters with no actual vocal talent basically have to trust others to be their voices. Me being who I am, my mind took that to a dark place and this story was the result.

Be My Voice

Wes couldn't help but notice the guy staring at him.

Of course, everyone in the club was staring at him. He was up on stage belting out a karaoke version of Bonnie Raitt's "I Can't Make You Love Me," after all. Spotlight was trained on him, so for the moment he was the center of attention.

Still, even with all the eyes turned his way, it was the stare of the guy in the corner that weighed on him the heaviest. Maybe it was the big brown mole on the side of the guy's nose that made him stand out in the crowd, or the intensity of the hunger in his eyes as he focused his gaze on Wes like a laser beam. Whatever the case, it made Wes uncomfortable enough that he reconsidered doing a second number.

Stepping down off the stage, he handed the microphone over to some nelly queen who went straight into "I Will Survive." Way to reinforce the stereotype! Wes made his way to the bar and ordered a beer. It was warm and flat, but he drank it anyway.

People didn't come to Rear Entrance for the drinks; they came here for…well, other things.

Speaking of which, the guy with the mole was still checking him out hard. Not Wes's type at all, so he just ignored the scrutiny and scanned the crowd for something a little more his taste.

And found it over by the pool tables.

A bit older, a little gray around the temples, but a lean body and plump sensuous lips. He leaned casually against the wall, sipping from a bottle of beer, giving the impression that he couldn't care less how he looked, which probably meant he cared a great deal.

Wes ambled over, trying to appear nonchalant and not like a predator on the prowl. He sat down on a nearby stool and pretended to watch a game between two men in leather pants. He was trying to come up with the perfect opening line when the older man leaned toward him and said, "You've got a beautiful singing voice."

Wes looked over at him, flashing his most charming smile. "Well, thanks. I'm not all that good, but I appreciate the compliment."

"No, really you are," the man said, stepping closer, having to practically shout to be heard over a drag queen mangling an Alicia Keys tune. "I've been to a lot of karaoke nights here, and usually it's just one butcher job after another, but you've got actual talent."

"Hey, you're not an agent, are you?"

The man laughed and held out a hand. "Afraid not. Name's Tom, actually in the construction business."

Ah, butch. Wes liked that. Tom had a firm handshake, callused fingertips, obviously a man who worked with his hands. Wes liked that even more. He introduced himself and made a show of finishing off his beer.

"Want another drink?" Tom asked.

"Sure."

"Okay, I'll go grab you one. Don't move, promise?"

"I'm planted right here in this spot 'til you get back," Wes said with a wink, knowing that this was a done deal.

Tom hurried off toward the bar, and Wes admired the man's bubble butt stuffed into tight jeans. Glancing back toward the stage he saw that a guy and his hag were now fumbling their way through "Don't Go Breaking My Heart." They were obviously on the far side of drunk, slurring the lyrics until the song was basically unrecognizable. Regardless, the crowd seemed to be having a good time, cheering and laughing and—

But not everyone in the crowd was focused on the stage. The guy in the corner, the one with the mole, was still staring at Wes. He didn't even seem to be blinking, a real psycho kind of stare. Wes was used to being looked at in clubs, he was cute and he knew it, but this was a bit unnerving. He imagined this was how a mountain lion stared at a gazelle before pouncing.

Did mountain lions hunt gazelles? Hell, Wes didn't know, he didn't watch too much Animal Planet, preferring Logo and Spike TV. Whatever the case, he felt like the guy with the mole was preparing to pounce.

And in fact, when Wes looked back over, the guy was making his way across the club toward him, a feminine swish to his walk. Great, just what Wes needed. He wasn't in the mood to have to shake off some creepy fag tonight.

Wes was mentally constructing the perfect zinger with which to shoot the guy down when Mr. Mole, as Wes was starting to think of him, came up and held out a piece of paper. All without a word. Interesting ploy, one he hadn't encountered before, but maybe for the socially inept a nonverbal approach might be best.

Assuming the paper contained Mr. Mole's phone number, Wes just shook his head and said, "No thanks."

Not to be dissuaded, the guy continued holding out the paper, waving it in Wes's face. Wes took the paper, but instead of reading what was on it, he just crumpled it up and tossed it on the floor. "Sorry, not interested."

And that was when Mr. Mole spoke...or tried to. He opened his mouth but all that came out was a bunch of garbled, indecipherable gibberish. Sort of like the way the adults talked on Charlie Brown, but more guttural. There were no actual words in the mix that Wes could make out.

Jesus Christ, is this guy a retard? Wes thought, getting up from the stool and taking a step away from Mr. Mole. The guy lunged forward, grabbing Wes's shoulders with surprising strength. He kept repeating the same sounds over and over, practically screaming them in Wes's face, and they seemed *almost* to be words. *Eee nine boys, eee nine boys, eee nine boys...*

"Hey, is this guy bothering you?" Tom asked, returning with the beer.

Wes shook Mr. Mole off him. "Yes, he really is."

"Take a hike, freak." Tom planted a hand on Mr. Mole's chest and shoved hard, sending the guy crashing into one of the pool tables, knocking some of the balls out of position. The two guys in leather pants cursed at him.

"Let's get out of here," Wes said, putting an arm around Tom's waist. "It's getting a bit too crowded in here."

Tom glared at Mr. Mole, an obvious threat in his eyes. "Couldn't agree more."

***

Wes thought that maybe he owed Mr. Mole a thank you. If he hadn't run Wes and Tom out of the club, they would probably have spent another half hour of inane getting-to-know-ya chitchat before getting down to the real crux of the matter: your place or mine?

But once they got out in the parking lot, all pretense was dropped and they settled on Wes's apartment since it was closer and Tom said his place was such a pigsty that he didn't like having people over. Wes translated that to mean Tom was possibly married or at least had a live-in girlfriend, but that was okay. Wes preferred his own place anyway.

"Wanna go together in my car?" Tom asked.

Wes translated that to mean, *Wanna give me a hand job in the car on the way over?* Wes could be down with that. "Sounds like a plan."

Tom was parked on the far side of the gravel lot, and the loose stone crunched under their feet with a sound not unlike autumn leaves. At midnight it was still early for the club crowd, so they passed no one else in the parking lot. Well, there was one car with fogged-over windows that rocked gently, but that was to be expected.

Tom drove a brand new Lexus, very nice, and as they approached the vehicle, Tom suddenly grabbed Wes and slammed him against the side of the car, planting a rough kiss on his mouth. Wes could feel the other man's stubble rubbing abrasively against his face, and he liked the way it felt. The smell of testosterone was heavy in the air like smoke, and he felt himself stiffening in his pants. He pressed against Tom's body to make sure the other man felt it too.

"I could just take you right now," Tom said in a husky voice, breaking the kiss.

"I only live five minutes away. We'll have a lot more room to play, and I have a few toys you might find interesting."

Tom made a sound deep in his throat that was part growl, part sigh. "Then let's not waste anymore time."

As Wes started around to the passenger's side of the car, Tom bent to unlock the driver's door. And that was when the shadow bolted out from behind the pick-up parked next to the Lexus.

It all happened so fast that Wes barely had time to register any of it. He heard the crunch of hurried footsteps, turned to see a flash of something silver, and then suddenly Tom had a gaping crimson grin below his jaw. He grasped at his throat and blood poured between his fingers and saturated the front of his T-shirt. He opened his mouth but nothing came out by a high-pitched whistling, the sound of the wind through a graveyard at midnight. He took a step toward Wes, his eyes imploring, then dropped to his knees before topping over on his side.

For a moment, Wes was too stunned to react. He couldn't move, couldn't even think. Then the shadow stepped closer, into the light thrown by the nearest pole light, and Wes gasped when he saw that it was Mr. Mole, holding a bloodied pocketknife.

His paralysis broken, Wes roared and charged the man, intending to tackle him and pummel his face until it was unrecognizable. However, the plan didn't quite work out that way. Instead, Mr. Mole punched Wes hard in the nose.

Only that wasn't exactly the case, either. Mr. Mole just held his fist out and Wes ran straight into it. His feet skidded on the gravel and he fell backward, banging his head on the driver's side window of the Lexus, shattering the glass.

There was a bright flash of pain, colors exploding before his eyes like a July 4th fireworks display, then blackness.

***

When Wes regained consciousness, there was no disorientation, no moment where he wasn't sure where he was or what had happened. The memory of

Tom with his throat slashed was vivid, the pain of Mr. Mole's fist slamming into his nose and then Wes's head cracking against the window of the Lexus could still be felt. He immediately took stock of his current situation.

He was in a dark room, the only light coming from the dim bulb of a lamp in the corner. There seemed to be no windows, and the floor was cement. The ceiling was high with various pipes running in maze-like configurations. Wes was sitting in what seemed to be an old kitchen chair, his ankles strapped to the front legs and his arms pulled painfully around the back of the chair and bound with what felt like electrical tape. Something that tasted like old gym socks smelled was stuffed in his mouth, more tape covering that.

Mr. Mole was squatting on the floor in front of him.

Wes began to buck in the chair, making muffled grunting noises behind the gag, but all he succeeded in doing was scraping the chair across the floor a couple of inches. He was securely bound, and he felt fear drawing his scrotum up close to his body even as a cold sweat began to slide down his forehead into his eyes, burning like acid. He had no idea how long he'd been unconscious. Had anyone yet found Tom's body in the parking lot of Rear Entrance? Or had Mr. Mole disposed of the body somehow? Was anyone looking for Wes?

Mr. Mole hopped to his feet in a single fluid motion and stepped closer. He reached into his pocket and Wes cringed back as far as he could, expecting to see the flash of the switchblade again. But instead Mr. Mole brought out a crumpled piece of paper and shoved it in Wes's face. It was the same paper he'd tried to give Wes back at the club. There seemed to be a note scrawled in shaky handwriting, but Wes turned his head away from it.

Mr. Mole backhanded Wes so hard across the face that he felt like his right eye was going to fall right out of its socket. The blow reignited the pain both in his nose and the back of his head, and he felt lightheaded, afraid for a moment that he was going to pass out. But he managed to hang on, and Mr. Mole was holding out the paper again. "eee id, eee id," he was saying over and over. At first Wes just shook his head, but then he thought he was beginning to understand what his captor was trying to say. Could 'eee id' be 'read it'?

As if in confirmation, Mr. Mole grabbed Wes's hair like he was trying to snatch him bald and jerked his head up, holding it steady while he held the paper right in front of his face. "eee id! eee id!" Having no other choice, Wes squinted past the pain and the dimness to make out the words on the paper.

My name is not important. What is important is what I do. And what I do is write songs. Music and lyrics. I write songs that explore universal themes of loss and longing, songs that get right to the heart of the human experience, songs that capture feelings most people can't put into words. Some might call it egotism, but I know I have a gift for songwriting that is practically unrivaled. Unfortunately, I cannot give voice to these songs myself due to the fact that I was born without a tongue. Not a common deformity, and there isn't much that can be done for it. There's no such thing as a prosthetic tongue. And it renders me incapable of taking my songs from just words and notes on a page and turning them into anthems for a generation. I have of course tried sending my songs to various record labels, figuring they could pair up my songs with the right singers to truly do them justice. I am sad to say that by and large my genius has yet to be recognized, although one of my songs was

That was where the note ended, and Wes looked up at Mr. Mole with questioning eyes. Mr. Mole nodded with a look of understanding and flipped the paper over, revealing the rest of the message.

bought last year by Starbright Records. And they proceeded to ruin it. They gave it to some teen pop princess with a voice like nails down a chalkboard to record, and they changed the music so that what was meant as a heartfelt ballad became some techno dance thing. The meaning and power of the song was lost, and it convinced me that if my music is to reach people and inspire them, I'll have to find the perfect voice myself. So I went on a search, and then last month I saw you at karaoke night at the club. Your voice has such passion and depth to it, the more I listened, the more I became convinced you were the one I was looking for. And so I have come back to karaoke night tonight in the hopes that you will be here. And if you are, if you are reading this, I ask this of you – be my voice.

When he finished reading the note, Wes stared up at Mr. Mole for a moment then broke into laughter. It was muffled by the gag, but his entire body shook with the intensity of his mirth. This was almost too ridiculous to believe. So this little twerp had kidnapped him not for some psycho-sexual reason but so that he could force Wes to sing his sappy little songs?

Not that it would have been *better* if Wes had been kidnapped for some psycho-sexual reason, but at least more understandable. Not quite such a farce.

The humor of the situation dried up, however, when Wes thought again of Tom. True, Wes hadn't known the man very well but he'd seemed like he was going to be one hell of a fuck, and now he was lying dead somewhere. And Wes could very well be joining him soon. Thinking about it in those terms made his predicament seem much less farcical in nature.

Mr. Mole knelt down in front of him, placing his hands on Wes's shoulders and squeezing. The man's expression was imploring, almost desperate. *"eee nine boys, eee nine boys..."*

Be my voice. That was what the guy was saying. Be my voice.

Wes was close to laughing again, but he swallowed it back. Laughter in the face of this lunatic wouldn't exactly be the smartest response. If Wes wanted to get out of this, he had to use his brain, be cleverer than his captor.

Forcing himself to be calm, trying to arrange his face into an expression at once scared and eager, he nodded, taking into his gag. Mr. Mole seemed pleased, then reached out and yanked the duct tape off Wes's mouth. Wes always sported a neatly trimmed mustache and goatee, and much of the hair was ripped out by the tape, a burning fire that engulfed the lower half of his face. Tears welled in his eyes as he spit the stained rag out of his mouth. He didn't even want to contemplate what it was stained with.

Wes gasped, gulping air like water, then screamed as loud as he possibly could, straining so that veins stood out like ropes in his neck. "SOMEBODY HELP ME! THIS GUY IS FUCKING CRAZY! HE'S HOLDING ME AGAINST MY WILL! SOMEBODY PLEASE HELP ME! CALL THE—"

Mr. Mole backhanded him again, this time with even greater force, causing Wes to bit down deep into his tongue, the sickly sweet taste of his own blood filling his mouth and coating the back of his throat. He gagged on it, coughing up blood and bile.

One side of Mr. Mole's mouth rose in a half-smile and he shook his head, as if to say, *You naughty boy.* He stepped back into a shadowy corner of the room, returning a moment later pulling a dry erase board on wheels. Taking up a blue marker, he began writing on the board, the faint *squeak* drilling into Wes's brain.

What Mr. Mole wrote on the board was: *Scream all you want. No one can hear you here.*

It was dialogue out of some really cheesy thriller. And maybe just as fictitious. Perhaps Mr. Mole was just saying that—or *writing it*—to keep Wes quiet. Then again, if it weren't true, would he have removed the gag at all? Either way, Wes had to try. He began screaming again, trying to project his voice through the ceiling, through the walls, out to whoever may be near enough to hear him. Mr. Mole stood there with his arms folded, that half-smile frozen on his lips. Wes wasn't sure how long he screamed, but he kept it up until his voice failed and his throat felt as if he'd been gargling broken glass.

Mr. Mole stepped behind Wes then came back around with a tall glass of water, a comical curlicue straw sticking out of it. He held it out to Wes, who didn't hesitate. He wrapped his lips around the straw and sucked the lukewarm liquid into his mouth eagerly, trying to quench the fire in his throat. It only succeeded a little, the glass drained much quicker than he would have liked.

When Wes was done, Mr. Mole patted him on the head like a dog then went back to the dry-erase board, writing a longer message under the first.

Now that you've got that out of your system, I'll let you rest your voice. Later I'll bring you some food, and tomorrow we will really get started. I have a feeling we're going to make beautiful music together.

And with that, Mr. Mole left the room, flipping a switch on his way that extinguished the lamp in the corner, plunging Wes into total darkness.

***

Several hours later Mr. Mole spoon-fed Wes a bowl of bean with bacon soup, as if Wes were an infant in his high chair. Wes briefly considered refusing to eat, going on a hunger strike, but he'd simply been too hungry to resist the enticing aroma of the soup. And bean with bacon wasn't even something he normally liked. Wes had always been a slave to his appetites, however. He would never have made it as Gandhi.

When Wes wasn't chewing and swallowing, he kept up a constant chatter. He thought he'd read in a magazine article once that kidnap victims should try to engage their captors as much as possible, get them to see the victims as real people with real lives. He didn't remember if the article reported that this tactic worked or not, but he was willing to try pretty much anything at this point.

"You know, I bet my mother is worried sick about me. I don't still live with her or anything—I mean, I'm not a loser—but we're pretty tight. I visit most every Sunday. My father died several years ago, you see, and I don't have any brother or sisters, so I'm all my mom has. I hate to think of the pain it would cause her if anything happened to me."

This elicited no reaction from Mr. Mole.

"You don't have to do this, you know. I mean, you seem like a decent guy, not a violent type. What you did to Tom…well, I'm sure you were just confused. Maybe you even saw him shove me up against the car and thought he was attacking me, thought you were protecting me. I could explain that to the cops."

Mr. Mole shook his head and chuckled.

"I'd love to hear your songs, I bet they're just amazing. I'd be honored to sing them for you, no doubt about it. It's really not necessary to keep me all tied up like this. I mean, I *want* to do it, I want to be your voice. Honest and truly."

This was greeted with a smirk that seemed to say, *Nice try.*

"Did you know I have pets? Of course you didn't. I have a dog, a Golden Retriever, two cats and an aquarium full of fish. There's no one to feed them with me being...away. I'm afraid they'll all starve to death."

This last desperate attempt to somehow connect with Mr. Mole got the most reaction. His eyes filled with what looked like genuine sympathy and he said, "*ah-wee.*" *Sorry.*

Not sorry enough to let Wes go, apparently. When Wes finished his soup, Mr. Mole went back to the board, where he'd erased the earlier messages, and wrote, *Tomorrow we will begin.*

And left.

***

Wes didn't think it would be possible to sleep bound to the chair as he was, but eventually he drifted off. He dreamed that he was dancing with Tom at Rear Entrance, blood constantly pumping from the slit in the older man's neck. It had made such a puddle on the dance floor that they kept sliding in it. Mr. Mole was up on stage, singing a popular Miley Cyrus song in his mangled, mush-mouth voice, coming out something like, "*ah-ee ew-eh-a.*" Tom asked for a kiss and Wes leaned forward, but instead of putting his lips on Tom's mouth, he put them over the vertical slash below the man's Adam's apple, thrusting his tongue deep into the wound, lapping up the blood as if he were drinking from a water fountain. It tasted sweet, like a soda with too much sugar in it, and Wes put his hand on Tom's face and forced the man's head back, causing the wound to tear open even wider, more blood gushing into Wes's waiting mouth—

A light slap pulled Wes from the dream. He experienced a half a second of relief at being freed from the disturbing nightmare, but then he found himself wanting to go back to it because it was less disturbing than his reality.

His chin was resting on his chest, and when he raised his head he cried out, his neck was so stiff. His entire body was achy and sore, and he felt like crying.

The lamp was back on, and on the board was written, *Rise and shine, time to get to work.* In front of Wes's chair/prison was a card table on which sat a tape recorder. One of the rectangular boxy kinds, the ones that used cassette tapes. So this was Mr. Mole's recording studio, huh? No fancy digital equipment here, just the very basics. Next to the tape recorder was a stack of sheet music, lyrics printed underneath the notes.

Mr. Mole stood by the table, a leather strap over his shoulder holding an acoustic guitar against his back. With a bright smile, he pointed first at the sheet music then at Wes.

"I need to use the bathroom," Wes said, and it was not just a ploy. His bladder felt like it were about to burst.

Mr. Mole shook his head, pointed back at the sheet music.

"I need to take a piss! We're not doing anything unless I do that first."

For a minute Mr. Mole's face got so red it looked like steam was going to shoot out of his ears like a cartoon character, but then he nodded and walked around behind Wes. He returned with the empty glass that had held the water last night, only now minus the curlicue straw. He knelt down in front of Wes, undid the man's fly and let his flaccid penis flop out. Positioning the glass under Wes's hose, Mr. Mole looked up expectantly.

"You've got to be fucking kidding me. Surely you don't expect me to take a leak in a glass."

Mr. Mole shrugged and started to take the glass away, but Wes said, "No, no, I'll do it."

He closed his eyes and relieved himself into the glass. It was humiliating, degrading, but it would be more humiliating if he wet his pants. He didn't even want to think about what would happen when he had to take a dump.

When he was done, Mr. Mole tucked him in and zipped him back up. Placing the glass, now filled three-quarters with urine, on the table next to the recorder, he again pointed at the sheet music, pulling the guitar around to the front, preparing to play.

Wes looked up at his captor and felt an all-consuming rage overwhelm him. It pushed everything aside—the soreness of his body, the fear, the humiliation—and that was good. He wanted to hold on to this feeling because it felt empowering.

"And what if I refuse? What if I won't be your little mockingbird? If you kill me, you'll never get my voice."

Mr. Mole was still for a moment, deathly still, then he grabbed the glass and flung the contents in Wes's face. His own reeking piss splashed into his mouth, his eyes, dripping from his hair. Then Mr. Mole brought the glass down hard on Wes's right knee, causing the glass to shatter. It felt to Wes as if his kneecap shattered as well, and shards of glass poked up from his flesh, blood seeping out.

The pain was like an atomic explosion in his knee, radiating up throughout his entire body. He screamed, tears coming to his eyes and trailing down his cheeks to mix with his urine. Multi-colored spots floated across his vision and he thought for a moment he was going to pass out, he hoped he would, but blessed unconsciousness remained elusive. He sobbed, blubbering, "Okay, okay, whatever you say, man." His resolve and rebellion had lasted exactly thirty seconds.

Mr. Mole patted Wes on the cheek — *Good boy* — but did not remove the glass embedded in Wes's knee. Wes bit into his bottom lip, not wanting to give Mr. Mole the satisfaction of hearing him whimper. But whimper he did, and much more. Snot poured from his nose as he bawled like he hadn't since he was a toddler. His body was racked with shivers so severe it was almost like convulsions.

Mr. Mole waited patiently until the episode had passed. Once Wes's sobs tapered off and he seemed to regain his composure (as much as one could when tied to a chair with a busted knee and his face coated with snot and piss), Mr. Mole once again indicated the sheet music. He was single-minded, Wes had to give him that.

Wes merely nodded, too exhausted and in too much pain to put up any more of a fight.

A delighted smile lighting up his face, Mr. Mole pressed the RECORD button on the recorder, took a moment to tune up his guitar, then started strumming a slow tune. Wes squinted down at the sheet music, following along with the notes to get his cue for when to start singing.

"Love...love is in the air. Love is everywhere. So please do not be scared...of loooove...."

Jesus Christ, he thought. This was one of the songs Mr. Mole thought were so powerful they were going to change the world? This piece of trite, simplistic garbage? "Row Your Boat" had more depth than this.

But it wasn't important, Wes would just do what was demanded of him, he'd sing the song, he'd sing any songs put before him, try to appease this crazy bastard and hopefully get out of this thing without any more damage. If he could just—

Mr. Mole suddenly stopped playing and backhanded Wes across his left cheekbone. He tilted his head like a quizzical dog then backhanded Wes again, almost like an afterthought. Wes's head rocked back and he started to cry again.

Going back to the dry-erase board, Mr. Mole wrote, "*Sing right!*"

"You're out of your fucking mind," Wes spat. "I'm doing what you want me to do."

Mr. Mole began writing again. *WITH FEELING!!!!! SING WITH FEELING!!!!*

"I'm doing the best I can, you sadistic prick!"

Reaching into his back pocket, Mr. Mole pulled out a switchblade. The one he'd used on Tom? Wes couldn't be sure, but he thought he noticed rust-colored stains on the blade as Mr. Mole rushed forward and thrust the thing out toward Wes's face. He gasped and recoiled his head as much as possible, the very tip of the blade coming to stop less than a quarter of an inch from Wes's right eye. The message

Mr. Mole was sending was clear: *You don't need your eyes to sing.*

Mr. Mole returned the switch blade to his back pocket, turned off the recorder and rewound the tape back to the beginning. Pressing RECORD again, he started playing the tune again, his expression hard and frightening in the dim light.

Wes licked his lips, praying silently to God to give his voice strength. He was so petrified he didn't know how he was going to manage to keep his voice from cracking, but he had to do it, he had to please this lunatic standing before him. Taking a deep breath, Wes looked down at the sheet music and sang.

"Love...love is in the air. Love is everywhere. So please do not be scared...of love. Love...love is everything. Love is why I sing. I look at you and dream...of love..."

The song went on like that, the melody monotonous, the lyrics ridiculously amateurish. He kept bracing himself for more abuse from Mr. Mole, but he was allowed to sing the song all the way through this time. When he was done, Mr. Mole turned off the recorder, then looked down at him for a moment, considering, then he shrugged with one shoulder as if to say, *It'll have to do.*

"Please, can I have some water?" Wes said, not liking the pleading whine he heard in his voice. "Something to eat? I sang your song for you, please...I'm so thirsty."

Mr. Mole shook his head, reaching down and removing the top piece of sheet music to reveal the next. There seemed to be about twenty of them in the stack.

"I'll sing all your songs, just please get me some water first. I'm begging you."

Mr. Mole kicked out with his foot and caught the side of Wes's injured knee, driving a shard of glass even deeper. Wes screamed and leaned forward as far as his bonds would allow and threw up all over his lap.

He let his head hang down, his eyes closed, weeping quietly now. He could hear the faint *squeak* as Mr. Mole wrote something on the board, but he did not look up. Not until Mr. Mole grabbed his hair and forced him to look.

I make the rules here, and you'll have to sing for your supper…or breakfast, as it were.

And so Wes sang…
And sang…
And sang…

***

Time ceased to mean anything for Wes after a while. With no windows, no clock, nothing to indicate what time of day it was, it was hard for him to be sure just how much time was passing. Still, he thought he'd been strapped to the chair for close to two weeks.

For the first few days Mr. Mole had fed him on a semi-regular basis, but that became more sporadic as time went on. He stopped offering Wes glasses to pee in, and on about the third day Wes soiled himself when he could hold it in no longer. Mr. Mole did not clean it up, nor did he tend to his captive's wounds. Wes's knee had swollen to the size of a grapefruit and he could practically feel infection coursing through his veins.

Mr. Mole made him sing those horrible songs over and over for hours on end. If he didn't do it to Mr. Mole's liking, he'd be rewarded with a fist to the eye or a swift kick to the groin. It seemed like it would never end, that it would just go on like this forever and ever...

Until the day Wes couldn't sing anymore. He tried, but his throat was raw and scratchy, his tongue felt like a dried out piece of sponge, and all that came out when he opened his mouth was a raspy croak. He cleared his throat, tried to work up some saliva, and made another attempt.

Another *failed* attempt.

Wes flinched, expected to be punched or pinched or kicked or bludgeoned in some way. When nothing happened, he looked up at Mr. Mole.

Who was simply standing there, his eyes brimming with what looked like sorrow. *"ear un ear,"* he said.

Wes had been listening to the man's gibberish enough that he thought he was getting good at translating.

We're done here.

"I can do it," Wes said desperately, his voice thin and shaky. "I just need some time to rest up my pipes, that's all. I swear, I can still sing for you. I can still be your voice."

Mr. Mole shook his head sadly then went to the board. *I'm afraid you're of no more use to me.*

Wes would have cried, but the fever that burned in him seemed to evaporate all his tears before they had a chance to fall. He watched in mute horror as Mr. Mole pulled out his switch blade and came toward him.

He didn't struggle, he didn't plead. He simply closed his eyes and waited.

***

Byron was elated.

This was the first time he'd ever performed in front of an audience, and he'd been terrified when he first got on the small stage of the coffee house, but when he'd started in on "The First Cut is the Deepest", he'd simply let go of all his fear and gotten lost in the music.

It was open mic night, which meant he could do only a three song set, but he could have gone longer, and he think the audience would have liked that as well. The applause he received was enthusiastic and seemingly sincere. It was a better high than any drug could give.

Carrying his guitar with him, Byron climbed down off stage, smiling as people he passed complimented him on his performance. His ego was being stroked to full erection, and he suddenly found himself wondering if maybe he should try out for the gig at the bar near his apartment. It didn't pay much, but he might just have a shot at it.

Sitting his guitar at his table, Byron went to the counter to order a coffee, and that was when he noticed the man staring at him. He was sitting alone in one of the comfy chairs, sipping a tea, his eyes trained on Byron and not wavering even when Byron noticed the scrutiny.

Byron smiled and waved. He was feeling in a generous mood and the guy was kind of cute.

Except for the mole on the side of his nose.

A small flash piece of the uncomfortable aftermath of a sexual adventure. I cannot remember the actual genesis of this idea, but I find it darkly amusing.

After

The bedroom was silent. Hank, still naked, sat on the bed with his back propped against the headboard. Lisa had pulled on her nightgown and was at the vanity, staring at her reflection in the mirror as if studying a stranger's face. Zed had left a little over half an hour ago, and neither Hank nor Lisa had spoken in that time.

Finally Hank swallowed hard enough to make an audible *click*, the small sound startling Lisa, and said, "You okay, babe?"

She nodded, picking up a brush and running it through her straight blonde hair. "Mmm-hmm."

"You sure?"

"I said I was, didn't I?" she said, a brittle edge to her voice.

Hank shifted uncomfortably on the mattress, pulling the sheet up to his waist as if overcome by a sudden bout of modesty. As if he and Lisa hadn't been sharing an apartment and a bed for nearly a year.

"Did you enjoy it?" he asked.

Another mute nod, then, "It was...fun."

"Yeah, fun. Not exactly what I had expected."

"You can say that again."

The threesome had been Lisa's idea. It had shocked Hank; she'd always seemed so reserved sexually. Then during a conversation about how they could spice up their lovemaking, she'd admitted she'd always fantasized about getting it from two guys at once. It wasn't ideal, Hank would have preferred a threesome with another chick, but he had to admit that the notion of watching Lisa getting nailed by someone else turned him on. Like live, interactive porn.

And so they'd found Zed. On an Internet website, although they'd met with him in person several times for coffee and conversation before deciding to go all the way. He seemed a nice enough guy, a couple of years younger than Hank and Lisa, fit and handsome.

And as it turned out, hung like a fucking horse. He and Hank had taken turns drilling Lisa in every conceivable position, sometimes one of them fucking her while she sucked the other off. It had been going great until Zed revealed he swung both ways and wouldn't mind messing around with Hank as well.

Of course, Hank had balked at first, but the suggestion had really gotten Lisa's engine revving to a degree he'd never seen before. She'd practically begged Hank to give it a try, going so far as to promise that she'd let him do her in the ass and she'd swallow the next time she blew him.

Still Hank had resisted, but then he figured, what the hell? This was just a one-time deal, after all, and if it got Lisa all hot and bothered…it wasn't as if anyone else ever had to know. So he'd done it, at Lisa's urging…

But now she was giving him the cold shoulder.

"Babe, talk to me," Hank said.

Lisa put the brush down very deliberately and met Hank's eyes in the mirror, as if not quite able to meet his gaze directly. "I just...I can't get the image of you two together out of my mind."

"I thought it was what you wanted."

"So did I, it's just that...I mean, it wasn't exactly how I'd pictured it was going to be."

"Babe, the only reason I did it was because you asked me to."

"I know, I know, it's just..."

"It's just what?"

Lisa turned toward him finally, the two of them face to face for the first time since Zed had left. Her eyes registered no recognition, as if she didn't even know who Hank was. "I'd just assumed that you were going to be the top."

Hank could think of nothing to say to that, so he said nothing as Lisa stood up and left the room.

This story was the result of a challenge from my partner. We were out having dinner, and he had taken the cloth napkin and folded it into what he called a Bishop's hat then took a photograph of it. We had just attended a writer's workshop, so he dared me to take that simple photograph and write a flash piece based on it. Not sure this was the story he was expecting. I thought it offered an interesting commentary on race and the perception that some have that racism is a thing of the past.

The Napkins

"Excuse me, Miss," Fred said in a gruff tone. When the pretty little white girl with the blonde ponytail passed him without even looking in his direction, he raised his voice. "I said EXCUSE ME!"

"Fred, please don't make a scene," his wife Carla said softly next to him.

The blonde stopped, sighed deeply, then turned back to Fred and his family. Her nametag read KATIE. "What can I do for you now?"

"We've been waiting to be seated for almost half an hour."

"Yes, we're very busy."

"But people who've come in after us have already been seated."

"As I've already tried to explain to you, those were smaller parties. We have to wait for a big enough table to open up for your group."

"There's only five of us!"

Carla put her hand on his arm, a simple gesture but after 20 years of marriage he knew it was her nonverbal way of saying *You're being an ass, let someone with a more level head handle this.*

"You'll have to forgive my husband," Carla said to the girl. "He becomes a beast when he's hungry. Can you tell us if it's going to be much longer?"

Katie sighed again, a sound that Fred was rapidly finding infuriating. "I think they're busing a table right now, I'll go check." Then she scuttled off once more.

"I can't believe this shit," Fred grumbled.

"Daddy, stop embarrassing us," said Debbie, his sixteen-year-old daughter. She seemed near tears. The other two members of their party—Fred and Carla's seven-year-old son Barry and Debbie's best friend Lisa—looked equally mortified. And they should have been mortified…but not over Fred's behavior.

"Don't you all see what's going on here?"

"Nothing is going on," Carla said, her voice low and lethal, "except that we're in a busy restaurant and are having to wait for a table."

"Come on, Carla, you're smarter than that. This isn't some hoity-toity French restaurant where you need reservations and a tie. It's a pizza joint, for Christ's sake. And you've seen all the lily white faces that have passed by and gotten tables since we got here."

"And you think they're purposely not seating us because we're black?"

"You don't?"

Carla rolled her eyes. "You know, not every white person you meet is a racist."

"No, just the racist ones."

"I'm so sorry about my dad, he's such a freak," Debbie mumbled to Lisa.

Fred was about to admonish his daughter for her disrespect when Katie returned with a scowl on her face. "Okay, we have a table open." Then she turned and started away again without waiting for Fred and his family. They hurried after her, Fred wearing a scowl of his own.

The table was in the back corner of the restaurant, just by the bathrooms, with barely enough room to cram all five of them. The children and Carla all sat down, but Fred remained frozen, staring at the tabletop. The salt and pepper, the parmesan, the silverwear…and the napkins.

"What the hell is that supposed to be?" he growled.

Katie followed his gaze then spoke as if she were talking to a mentally deficient child. "Those are napkins. You use them to wipe your hands and mouth."

"I know what napkins are, you twit."

"Fred," Carla said, and immediately started apologizing to the girl on her husband's behalf.

"Don't apologize for me," he said. "Look at how those napkins are folded."

"It's just decorative," Katie said with a sneer. "They're supposed to look like Bishop hats."

"Those are no Bishop hats."

Carla stared at the folded napkins then back up at her husband. "What are you talking about?"

"Look at those things, they look just like klan hoods."

The three children all sank down in their seats as if trying to disappear. Carla seemed speechless for a moment, which wasn't an easy feat, then said, "Fred, I think you're really reaching here. They're just folded napkins."

"Look at the other tables around us, the napkins aren't folded like this."

"We only fold the napkins when we're ready to seat someone," Katie said. "And if you continue to be belligerent, I'm going to have to call my manager."

"Don't bother, we're not staying."

"Fred, please," Carla started.

"Don't argue with me, we're not going to patronize an establishment that employs blatant bigots."

Against their protests, Fred ushered his family from the table and back through the restaurant.

***

Katie watched the nigger family leave, then with a self-satisfied smile she shook out the napkins and refolded them the usual way.

Flash fiction often is expected to have some kind of twist, or as I've heard some call it a "punch line," at the end. This is one where I really enjoyed the punch line I came up with. It originally appeared as part of Immure Spirits, *a digital collection released in 2011 by Creature House Publications.*

Anything

"Dear, do you know how you always say you'd do *anything* for me?"

I was sitting on the sofa watching a football game on television, home from work only fifteen minutes, when my wife surprised me with the question. Evelyn and I had been married only six months, still newlyweds, and the mere sight of her never failed to enflame my passion and sense of devotion. I turned off the game without hesitation.

"Of course, *anything*. There's nothing I wouldn't do for you."

She sat next to me and placed her hand on my knee, and my entire body was thrumming with what felt like an electrical current. "That's good to hear, and I think we're about to put it to the test."

"What do you mean?"

"There's something I need you to do for me, and it's not something you're going to enjoy doing. It's not something I enjoy asking you to do, but I must ask nonetheless."

A frown of concern on my lips, I scooted closer and put my arms around her. "Evelyn, honey, you're scaring me. Just tell me what it is you need me to do, and I'll do it."

"I need you to bury my father for me."

I don't know what I was expecting, but it certainly wasn't this. "What are you talking about? Your father's dead?"

"He's wrapped up in a tarp in the basement as we speak."

"Oh my God. Did you...I mean, what happened?"

Evelyn was chewing on her bottom lip, a nervous habit of hers I'd always found adorable. She gazed at me with such a look of naked desperation and fear that I felt my heart cracking like ice during a thaw. "I didn't kill him, if that's what you're thinking."

"Of course not, I would never think you capable of such an act."

"I just thought, what with the life insurance policy he recently took out, that you might think..."

"Never," I assured, holding her even tighter. "I know you and know you would never do anything like that. But I must ask, what did happen?"

"I can't tell you," she said, pulling away. "That's hard for me to say to you, you know I have never lied to you and I never will, but there are some things I just can't tell you. I simply ask you to trust that I didn't kill him."

"But who did? Evelyn, we should call the police."

"No! No police. I can't explain it, not now. Believe me when I say that there will be a time when I'll come clean with all the details, but for now I can only tell you that we can't call the police, and I need you to bury him."

My mind was reeling, this was just too insane. I knew I should grab the phone and call the authorities right away...and yet when I looked at my beautiful wife, I knew that I would do anything she asked.

***

Getting him out of the basement wasn't really all that hard. Evelyn's father was a small man, and he weighed very little. I merely threw his tarp-wrapped form over my shoulder and carried him up. In the garage, I placed him in the trunk of my Cadillac along with a shovel, and then Evelyn and I drove away from our quiet neighborhood.

I wasn't really sure where we should bury him, but Evelyn suggested a spot deep in the woods on the edge of town. It was a place where we often liked to picnic, far off the beaten path and we rarely saw anyone else. I had a feeling that after tonight, I would no longer feel much like picnicking there.

Evelyn stood nearby, sniffling in the darkness, while I dug the hole. I don't know that I made it six feet, but it seemed plenty deep when I stopped, retrieved the body, and deposited it in the makeshift grave. Evelyn wept openly as I filled the hole back in with earth.

"Do you want to say anything?" I asked when I was done.

She merely shook her head then proceeded to kick leaves and pinecones over the grave to better conceal it.

The return trip was filled with tension and silence. Neither of us spoke until we were back at home, still sitting in the car, parked in the garage. I turned to her and said, "Honey, I have to know or it will eat at me forever, how did your father die?"

Evelyn took a deep breath and turned toward me. It was hard to make out her expression in the darkness, but she reached out and touched my face. "I would say by now, he has suffocated."

"What? I don't understand."

"He wasn't dead when you buried him. Only drugged and unconscious."

This wasn't possible, what she was telling me. I shook my head to refute it. "No, you told me —"

"I told you only that I didn't kill him, but I needed you to bury him. I never said he was dead; I have never lied to you and I never will."

The car seemed to be caving in around me, as if we were in one of those compactor machines that turned vehicles into little cubes. My breathing became labored and I felt trapped in a nightmare.

Oblivious to my emotional state, or perhaps not caring, Evelyn slid across the seat and kissed me on the cheek. "Dear, you always say you'd do *anything* for me, and tonight you proved it."

When I first met my partner, a Buddhist, I was impressed by his determination never to harm any living creature, not even a bug. That gave me the inspiration for this story, but I assure you I do not do the things that are done by the "booty-kiss's" partner in this one.

Cockroach Mecca

"So the place is nice enough and all," Earl said as he and his cousin scuttled across the kitchen floor toward the sink, "but I really don't see why you were so insistent I had to move here. I mean, the place I was crashing before…man, that place was heaven. A total dump, trash everywhere, it was like a twenty-four hour buffet. Look at this place…we're lucky to find a few crumbs here and there."

Carl just chuckled as the two started up the face of the counter. "You're missing the big picture, cuz."

"And what's that?"

"Okay, so your old place had plenty of food…but what was the mortality rate there?"

"I admit, wasn't the safest place to live. Got bombed a couple of times, the giants were always after us, stomping and squashing us whenever they could. Still, if you were smart and knew how to stay hidden when the lights were on, you could survive."

"Well, just you wait."

"What's that supposed to mean?"

The two had just crawled into the sink where a few crumbs lingered from last night's dinner dishes when the overhead light blazed to life, shedding a frosty glow over the kitchen. Earl started to dart away, but Carl said, "Where you going, cuz?"

"Here comes the giant, we have to get the hell out of here."

Carl just chuckled but refused to move. Every instinct Earl had told him he should run, but morbid curiosity—and considering that he was likely about be killed, *very* morbid—got the better of him and he stuck by his cousin's side.

The giant walked into the kitchen, and his size was massive even for a giant. His head almost brushed the ceiling, and his chest and shoulders were wide. A lot of weight he could put behind a squashing foot. Earl began to quiver right down to his antennae.

"Trust me," Carl whispered. "Just stand your ground."

The giant crossed to the sink, took a glass from the dish-drainer, then stood staring down at the cousins with a frown on his face.

This is it, Earl thought. *Last thing I'll see is that big fist crashing down at me. Or maybe he'll turn on the faucet and I'll wash away down the drain just like happened to my daddy.*

Though next to him his cousin remained relaxed and unconcerned, Earl tensed and started to pray when the giant reached down into the sink...

...but the man just tapped on the side of the sink, saying, "Shoo, bugs. I got to turn on the water, don't want to drown you."

Now it was Earl who frowned up at the giant. Was this some kind of trap? Didn't seem likely when the beast could simply kill them now, but instead he kept encouraging Earl and Carl to get out of the sink before he turned on the water. Most peculiar behavior.

Carl took a few more nibbles on the crumbs then began to leisurely crawl to the edge of the sink and up. Bemused, Earl followed. When they reached the countertop, Carl stopped and turned, just watching as the giant poured a glass of water and downed it in two big gulps. He then rinsed the glass, returned it to the drainer, then walked back out of the room.

"What the hell was that?" Earl exclaimed.

"That, cuz, was a booty-kiss."

"A what?"

"A booty-kiss. Some kind of eastern philosophy or something. Believes all life is sacred, even ours. Wouldn't harm a fly…and I mean that literally."

"So you're saying…"

"I'm saying we have the run of the place. Go where we want when we want, no more scurrying and cowering in the darkness. This guy won't do anything to us. No bombs, no thrown shoes, no flushing us down the toilet. I mean, last month this guy *accidentally* killed an ant by sitting a coffee mug down on it, and he actually cried. Can you imagine? A giant crying over an ant!"

Earl took a moment to really let it all sink in, and he felt something akin to awe coursing through his little black body. "This is too good to be true."

"I'd say the same thing if I hadn't been living it the past year."

"Well, I'm sold. Unpack my bags, I'm moving in."

"Good deal, but my suggestion is to try to be a little tight-lipped about this place."

"What do you mean?"

"The temptation is to go bragging to everybody about what a sweet setup we got here, but we have to be selective about who we tell otherwise the place will be overrun by every bug, spider, and housefly in the area."

"Gotcha. My lips are sealed."

six months later...

Carl and Earl huddled behind the big trashcan that sat by the backdoor. They had found a lone macaroni noodle hidden back here, and they were sharing it, trying to be quick before anyone else discovered them. They could hear the commotion in the kitchen, hundreds of bugs rampaging all over the place.

"Your lips are sealed," Carl said bitterly. "Yeah, right."

"Hey, I only told my mother. I had no idea she was going to blab it to the rest of the family, and then they'd blab it to all their friends."

"Well, thanks to you our little secret haven has become an overcrowded ghetto."

"It's still the safest place I've ever lived. I mean, all these bugs living here, and rarely does anyone die not from natural causes. Crowded or not, this place is still heaven."

Carl just grunted, the closest he could come to conceding that his cousin had a point. When the two had sated their hunger on the noodle, they crawled out from behind the trashcan and headed toward the kitchen table, wondering if they might find some dessert underneath it. Halfway there they ran into Judy, a sexy little roach that had moved in about four months ago. Both Carl and Earl had a massive crush on her, and she flirted shamelessly with both of them.

"Hey Judy," Earl said. "Coming back from under the table?"

"Sure am, sweet thing."

"Anything good there?" Carl asked, shoving his cousin aside.

"There is a bit of brownie under there, but you'll have to fight a mob to get at it."

Carl looked around to make sure no one was close enough to hear. "Well, I happen to know where there's a partially eaten macaroni noodle."

"Hey, I'm the one that found the noodle in the first place," Earl broke in.

"What does it matter which one of us found it?"

"You were just making it sound like you were doing her a favor by telling her, when I'm the one that did you the favor by telling you."

"If it wasn't for me, cuz, you wouldn't even be here, and there would be a lot more food to go around for us."

"Oh yeah, why don't you just take your —"

"Excuse me, fellas," Judy said, instantly gaining their attention. "I'd be extremely grateful to both of you if you'd show me where this feast is before someone else finds it and gobbles it up."

"Follow me," Carl and Earl said in unison.

They turned back toward the trashcan when the giant came out of the bedroom and into the kitchen. Several of the newer residents scampered for cover, a habit that took a while to break, but the long-timers just stayed where they were, staring up at the giant.

Giants actually. The booty-kiss had brought home another giant the previous night. This one wasn't as tall and slighter of build, but still towered high above.

"I don't like that new giant," Earl said softly.

Carl laughed and puffed out his chest, for Judy's benefit Earl was sure. "Don't be such a coward. You heard the booty-kiss last night, telling the smaller one to avoid hurting us."

"Yeah, but I don't like the way he looks at us."

As if on cue, the smaller giant turned his eyes on the trio and glared at them. Earl trembled, feeling more afraid than he had in the past half a year.

"Don't worry," Judy said, making Earl feel all the more pathetic, having to be comforted by a woman. "Even if the new giant did want to harm us, the booty-kiss would never allow it."

"I guess you're right."

"Of course we're right, cuz," Carl said. "Now stop being such a wuss, and let's go show Judy the grub."

They had just started forward again when the giants began to speak, their voices booming loud through the kitchen.

"I just have to go teach this private Yoga lesson," the booty-kiss said. "Shouldn't be gone more than an hour and a half. You sure you don't mind hanging out here 'til I get back?"

"Not at all. Just be quick, I miss you already."

The giants did that peculiar thing they sometimes did where they press their faces together, then the booty-kiss walked across the kitchen and into the living room. Skirting around the many bugs in his way, careful not to step on any.

At the front door he paused and called back, "Help yourself to anything in the fridge. And again, I'm sorry about all the bugs. I know it must seem awfully weird that I won't kill them, but..."

"It's okay, really," the smaller giant said. "I respect your beliefs."

"Thanks. I won't be long, promise."

Then the booty-kiss was gone. The smaller giant went to the window above the sink and looked out.

"We should go," Earl said. "Let's get behind the trashcan quick."

Carl laughed again. "What has gotten into you? Didn't you hear what the giants just said?"

"Yes, and I also saw that the smaller one had his fingers crossed the whole time."

"What does that have to do with—"

Carl was interrupted by the sound of gushing water and screams. The trio all turned toward the sink and saw that the smaller giant had turned on the faucet full-blast, the hot water apparently judging by the steam, and was washing all the bugs that had gathered in the sink down the drain. They screamed, they gasped, they gurgled, they pleaded for help. Earl found himself flashing back to the day his father died.

And the giant stood over the sink, staring down and laughing. "What's wrong, you critters can't swim? Well, so long you disgusting little fuckers."

Then, moving with a quickness that was unusual for a creature so large, the giant whirled around, grabbed the broom by the stove, and started stomping across the kitchen, crushing bugs underfoot even as he smashed down on others with the heavy broom.

I told you so were the words that came to Earl's mind, but what he said was, "RUN!"

Almost as if they were of one mind, Earl, Carl, and Judy all took off for the relative safety of the refrigerator, intending to seek shelter in its shadowy under-region. They had covered only half the distance when the broom came down on top of Carl and Judy. Earl heard their anguished screams, but he did not even pause to see if they had been killed or merely injured. He immediately changed course and headed for the kitchen table. Not as safe as the refrigerator, but definitely safer than being exposed out here in this linoleum wasteland. All around him bugs were dying. Friends, family, strangers. Blood and guts sprayed into the air as more and more were crushed under the tyrant's feet.

Earl made it to the table and was just allowing himself a small breath of relief when he heard the giant say, "Oh no you don't," and then the broom came sweeping at him from the side, catching him and dragging him back out in the open, tossing him onto his back. Earl twisted and squirmed for a minute, trying to roll himself back over. When he finally managed to regain his feet, he found himself alone. All the other bugs were either dead or had made it to a safe hiding place. It was just Earl...and the giant towering high above him.

The giant smiled, a malicious twinkle in his eye, but he did not speak. He just raised his leg.

The last thing Earl saw was that foot plummeting toward him like a crashing planet.

I was watching a lot of Twilight Zone *when I wrote this one, and I think you can definitely see the influence. It's a TZesque tale with a little bit of a Mark Gunnells twist.*

Sunday Bath

Emerson had just finished filling the tub when there was a knock at the bathroom door. Irritated, he opened the door and barked "What?" into his wife's face.

Dana stood there with her arms folded across her chest, a smirk twisting her thin lips. "The Internet is out again. I need you to fiddle with the wires like you did last time."

"Fine, but after my bath, okay?"

The smirk became a faux-pout. "But what am I supposed to do 'til then?"

"I don't know, Dana. Read a book, watch TV, clean the kitchen, have an affair for all I care. It's not like you do anything important on that computer anyway. Damn waste of time, is what it is."

"Oh, really? A waste of time? You mean like these Sunday afternoon soaks you take in the tub?"

"I told you, the baths help me relax."

"Well, the Internet helps me relax."

"Dana, please, I've already filled the tub and I don't want the water to get cold. I promise I'll check the modem's connection just as soon as I get done with my bath."

Dana laughed, the sound carrying a hint of schoolyard bully meanness. "I've never known a sixty year old man to be so in love with long baths. You're worse than a woman. You might as well add bubbles, bath salts, and get yourself one of those inflatable pillows."

Sighing, Emerson massaged his temples, combating the burgeoning headache that was starting to develop behind his eyes. "I don't ask for much, do I? Just one day out of the entire week that you'll let me relax in the tub without any interruptions or nagging. That's not unreasonable, is it?"

"Fine," Dana spat. "Go ahead and have your girlie bath."

After his wife stalked off down the hall, Emerson shut the door and twisted the lock. Stripping out of his clothes, he avoided looking at his reflection in the mirror. He was familiar enough with his naked body, with the liver spots and paunch that made him look four months pregnant, the wrinkly skin that hung down in places like empty knapsacks. Getting old was a bitch, especially when you were married to one. Although that wasn't really fair to Dana; he wasn't exactly the ideal husband. This was the life he'd chosen so he had no one to blame but himself.

Trying to put those thoughts out of his mind, he stepped into the tub. The water was lukewarm, not too hot, just the way he liked it. He let out a soft, purring moan as he stretched out, propping his head back against the rim of the tub. He closed his eyes and breathed in the silence. He knew somewhere out there Dana still grumbled and fumed, but not here, not in this place. His Sunday baths were a time of respite, of solitude, where he could recuperate from the stings and jabs of the everyday world. It wasn't enough, not nearly enough, but he made the most of the time he had.

Taking a deep breath and holding it, Emerson sank down until his head was submerged under the water. He stayed that way until he felt his lungs were burning from the need for oxygen, then he slowly let his entire body float back to the surface. Opening his eyes, he was temporarily blinded by the light, but then a cloud moved over the sun as if just for Emerson. Smiling wide, he flipped over and began to swim slowly toward the shore of Lake Wassoe.

It was a beautiful summer afternoon, slightly overcast with just a touch of a breeze. Maybe rain later in the evening, but not right now. Right now everything was perfect.

Including the young man that waited on the shore, stretched out on a towel, wearing nothing but a smile.

Emerson emerged from the water also naked, looking down at his firm, tanned body. No wrinkles, no spots, stomach flat and taut. The body of a sixteen year old.

"I've missed you," said the young man on the towel. "I feel like it's been years since I saw you last."

Emerson stretched out next to the young man. "It's been a week, Jeremy, just like always, but I know what you mean. We have to spend far too much time apart."

"If only..." Jeremy said no more, but he didn't have to. Emerson knew the taste of regret.

If only Emerson hadn't been afraid of his feelings when he'd met Jeremy the summer of 1967 when his family had vacationed at Lake Wassoe. If only they'd done more than just exchange a few chaste kisses on the shore of the lake. If only Emerson's family had returned to Lake Wassoe the next summer instead of choosing to vacation in the mountains. If only...

Maybe Emerson would have found the strength to defy the societal norms of the time, to be who he knew in his heart he was born to be. Maybe he wouldn't have spent his entire life living a lie, stuck in a bad marriage, afraid he'd waited too long to ever make it right. Maybe he would have been happy.

As it was, all that made life bearable were his Sunday baths, his all-too-brief visits with Jeremy.

"What are you thinking about?" Jeremy asked, running a finger lightly down Emerson's face and tracing his jaw line.

"Just about how happy I am here with you. How much I love you."

"And I love you."

They kissed then, deeply and passionately, falling back onto the towel. They made love the way they'd never had the courage to all those many summers ago. They started slow and gentle, but the intensity increased as they explored each other's bodies. There was hunger and need in each kiss, each caress, each thrust. They both climaxed several times before collapsing in a sticky, sweaty heap.

They lay together as the afternoon wore on, wrapped in one another's arms, talking about their lives—the way they'd turned out and the way they *wish* they'd turned out. Finally they settled into a comfortable silence as they let the wind wash over their bodies, the sun dipping toward the distant horizon. The world was utterly quiet for a while...

...until a loud knocking started echoing around the lake, seeming to come from all places at once.

"You have to go," Jeremy said. Not a question, but a statement full of sadness and longing.

Emerson kissed Jeremy three times, on the forehead, on the cheek, and on the lips. Just as he always did, a parting ritual. "Yes, but I will be back next Sunday."

"Promise?"

"Cross my heart."

And then Emerson stood, dashed across the shore and dove into the lake. He swam underwater for a bit, the knocking reaching him even submerged as he was, then started kicking upward, headed for the wavering light. He splashed to the surface—

—and found himself back in the tub, water sloshing over the rim to drench the floor. His body was once again old and frail.

"Emerson!" Dana said loudly, pounding on the door. "You've been in there nearly an hour and a half, you must be a shriveled up prune by now. I mean, even more so than you usually are. I've been patient, but how about you get your scrawny ass out of the tub and fix the Internet?"

Emerson had a moment of disorientation as he adjusted to being back here, but it passed. "Coming, Dana. Just let me get dried off and into some clothes."

"Well, hurry, I don't have all day."

With a weary sigh, Emerson got out of the tub.

***

The following Sunday, as Emerson headed for the bathroom, Dana, who was sitting at the computer desk in the living room updating her Facebook status, called, "Have a nice soak, want me to bring you some Calgon? It'll take you away."

Her brittle laughter followed him down the hallway, but he did not respond. In fact, he had spent the weekend trying to avoid conversation with his wife. He was a terrible liar, and he was afraid she'd be able to tell in his voice that something was wrong. He was going to have to tell her eventually, and soon, but he just didn't have the energy for the ensuing confrontation.

Not that it was his fault. When his boss, Mr. Stevens, called him into the office Friday afternoon, he'd made it clear Emerson was not being fired for poor performance. The company simply wasn't doing well, and they were having to downsize. More than a dozen people were terminated Friday. Emerson couldn't help but notice most of them were around his own age. Out with the old and all that. Sure, Emerson could take early retirement but he and Dana wouldn't be able to live off the measly Social Security check he'd get every month. He'd end up having to go out and get a part-time job just to supplement the income. And who was looking for a 60 year old part-timer?

But Emerson would worry about all that later. Now it was time for his Sunday bath.

He stripped as he filled the tub and then lowered himself into the lukewarm water. As always, he slid underneath and came back up at Lake Wassoe. When he joined Jeremy at the shore, he said nothing of his troubles. This was not a place for troubles; this was a place where all troubles melted away.

They made love again, then as if sensing Emerson's tension without being told, Jeremy had Emerson stretch out on his stomach and Jeremy massaged his back. The young man's fingers were masterful, and it was as if they were pulling all of Emerson's frustrations and uncertainties from his body where they floated away on the wind like dandelion fluff.

The inevitable knocking came much too soon.

"You have to go," Jeremy said.

Emerson sat up and looked back toward the lake. It's usually tranquil surface was quivering with the force of the knocking. Emerson took a deep breath and made a decision. "No."

Jeremy frowned. "What?"

"I said no, I'm not going back."

"I don't understand."

Emerson leaned forward and kissed Jeremy, then took his hand. "I'm going to stay here with you."

There was a war going on in Jeremy's eyes. Hope and joy battling it out with doubt and fear. "But...are you sure?"

"I've never been more sure of anything in my life. I am yours...if you want me."

"Of course I want you, it's just that...well, you understand where I am, right? What happened to me in the lake the summer after we met? You know that I'm—"

Emerson put a finger to the young man's lips to silence him. "I know, and I am ready to be with you."

The knocking continued, but the two men ignored it. Standing, clasping hands, they walked away from the lake.

This is my little take on how a writer's real life can seep into the fiction he is writing. It's not horror but I think a rather interesting tale. I've written other supernatural tales about Nigel, but this one remains my favorite.

Art Imitates Life

"How is everything, gentlemen?"

Greg Nigel sat his fork down very deliberately, wiping the corners of his mouth, before looking up at the waiter. "'How is everything?' Is that what you asked?"

"Uhm, yes, sir."

"Let's see...Kirk, is it? Well, Kirk, first of all, my dinner companion and I sat here for exactly fifteen and a half minutes before you ever showed up to take our drink order. We had to wait an additional eleven minutes and forty-five seconds before you took our meal order. The meal itself did not show up at the table for another fifty-two minutes. During all that time of waiting, we received no bread or rolls. We've been sitting here for over an hour and a half, and you have only bothered to refill our glasses twice. You've done an outstanding job, however, of making yourself scarce. And that only describes the shitty service we've received from you; that doesn't even get into this drek you are passing off as food at this establishment."

"Oh, I see, well, I guess, uh, if you're that unsatisfied, perhaps you might like to speak to the manager on duty." The waiter was already backing away from the table, the way someone might back away from a rabid animal.

"Yes, Kirk dear, why don't you run along and fetch someone with an IQ in the double digits."

The waiter turned and rushed into the back.

"Was that really necessary?" Paul Wells asked, refolding his napkin in his lap over and over. "The food wasn't that bad."

"Paul, honey, you are such a sweetheart," Nigel said, reaching under the table and squeezing Paul's knee. "But you simply cannot allow yourself to put up with shoddy service. If you don't complain, mediocrity is all you're ever going to get out of life. Trust me, to get the best there is, you have to be a total asshole."

"You should know."

Nigel glanced over his shoulder to see a round little man with thinning hair and an out-of-date suit scurrying in their direction. This could be none other than the manager.

"Howdy, fellas," the round man said, stretching out a damp hand. His cheeks were flushed and a single line of sweat trickled down his forehead. Obviously not a man who dealt with conflict well. "My name is Marvin; I'm the manager here. I understand you found your dining with us less than satisfactory."

"Yes," Nigel said in a pleasant tone, ignoring the proffered hand, "much the way I'm sure Jesus found hanging up there on that wooden cross less than satisfactory. And like Jesus, I've got a feeling the food I've eaten here will indeed rise again."

Paul was twisting his napkin, attempting to make some type of origami creation from it. His face was almost as red as Marvin's and his eyes were trained very keenly on his hands.

"Well, I'm sorry that our food was not to your liking," Marvin said, flustered, but also with an unmistakable note of indignation.

"I have a dog that eats his own feces. After forcing down my meal here, I'm beginning to think I'd rather eat his feces as well."

"Greg, please," Paul said, meeting Nigel's gaze with a look of desperate, hopeful pleading.

After a moment of silence, Nigel turned to Marvin and said, "May I have a comment card, please? I'd like to record my displeasure with your establishment."

"Certainly, certainly," Marvin said, bowing like a Japanese businessman. "And don't worry about the bill. The food is on the house tonight."

"I would imagine so. That'll be all, Marvin."

As the manager scurried back the way he'd come in search of a comment card, Nigel brushed a few crumbs from his shirt and took a final sip of his tea. "Well, what do you say we get going?"

"Aren't you going to wait for the comment card?" Paul asked, glowering across the table.

"No, not necessary. I've had my fun. A lesson: never start bitching until after the meal. That way, they can't spit in your food. Oh, come now, you really shouldn't look so sullen, Paul. It's not becoming on you."

"You shouldn't be such a fucking prick, Greg. It's not becoming on you."

"Quite the contrary," Nigel said, rising from the booth. "I think it suits me splendidly. Greg Nigel, a glorious prick, that's me."

As Nigel turned and headed for the door, Paul quickly dug in his pockets and threw two twenties on the table.

"You're always so serious," Nigel said as Paul caught up with him at the door. "You've got to learn to let loose every once in a while and have some fun."

"I guess belittling others and acting all superior just isn't my idea of a good time."

Nigel reached the Mustang and unlocked the passenger's side door, holding it open for Paul. "See, I can be a gentleman when I want to be."

"I know you can," Paul said. "You are so sweet and loving toward me; I just wish you could direct some of that tenderness toward others."

"Honey, it's enough of a struggle being sweet to one person. If I tried to spread it around, it'd probably kill me."

Paul slouched in the seat, arms folded across his chest, looking very much like a petulant child.

Nigel glanced around the parking lot to make sure no one was watching, then leaned over and ran his fingers through Paul's fine wheat-colored hair. "Besides, you're the only person I've ever met who deserved my tenderness. You're one of a kind."

Paul's eyes softened, and he allowed Nigel to kiss him, parting his lips slightly so Nigel could sneak in his tongue.

"Now, let's go home and make love," Nigel said, starting the car.

"Well, okay," Paul said with a wicked twist to his mouth. "You know I can't resist a glorious prick."

***

"You are unnecessarily cruel," Delano said. "Why must you torment them so before the kill?"

"Because it's fun," Sullivan replied simply, wiping blood from the corners of his mouth with his monogrammed handkerchief. "It brings me pleasure to play with them, build their hope then crush it, prolonging the pain for my own entertainment."

"You are a monster," Delano whispered.

Sullivan smiled wide, his fangs overhanging his full, luscious lips. "I am what you made me, old friend."

***

Nigel sat at his desk in one of the spare bedrooms, which he had converted into his office space. He eyes were glazed and staring into the portal of the screen, fingers flying over the word processor's keyboard like pale, tap-dancing spiders. He was unaware of the sound of the vacuum clearer downstairs, oblivious to the ache in his back from leaning forward in his chair. The room around him was insubstantial, and Paul's voice calling up the stairs was a distant echo that did not register in his ears. Nigel was not there in that room, he was through the portal of the screen before him, lost in that other world, the world he had created in his fiction.

Nigel had published ten novels to date, and his most recent, *No Laughing Matter*, was celebrating its third week at number one on the bestsellers list. The novel before that, a gothic ghost story entitled *Old Habits Die Hard*, was in its second month as a paperback bestseller. Nigel was riding a wave of success that had brought him wealth and prestige, and his publisher was anxious for his next piece of work.

Nigel's hands paused above the keyboard, fingers poised at the ready; he nibbled at his lower lip. His eyes ticked back and forth like one of those novelty cat clocks, then his hands dove down as if he had been waiting for some silent cue, lines of yellow type filling the black screen.

Nigel was currently writing the fourth book in his very popular Vampire Feast series, a series that detailed the exploits of the Vampire Sullivan, a character some critics had called the writer's "alter ego." This book, tentatively titled *Night Stalker*, was different than the others in that it was actually a prequel to the three that came before it, telling of the rift that developed between Sullivan and his maker, the Vampire Delano, causing the two to become bitter enemies.

"Greg," Paul said sharply, storming into the office.

Nigel slammed back into his seat as if thrown against the back of the chair. The portal closed, and the room around him began to gain more focus and clarity, reality reestablishing its hold. As always when this happened, Nigel let go of the fantasy with the greatest reluctance. He turned his eyes to Paul, anger simmering just below the surface.

"I have asked you not to barge in while I'm working, haven't I?" he said in a strained voice.

"Yes, but I've been calling you for the past ten minutes."

"I'm sorry, but you know how I get when I'm writing. All I ask is two and a half hours in the evening; is that too much?"

"Hello, Mr. Time Warp, check your watch. You've been at it for over four hours now."

Nigel glanced at the small digital clock on the corner of the desk and was stunned to see that Paul was right. Nigel had sat down at the word processor just before three in the afternoon; it was now a quarter past seven. Nigel scrolled up the screen to discover that he'd completed over twenty-fives pages of text. He had been in the zone, that mythical zone of creativity that came over him sometimes, milking the words from him and entrancing him in the magic of world-making.

"Wow, I didn't realize," Nigel said, his voice and facial expression softening. "I'm sorry, I didn't mean to get all snappish with you."

"It's okay; I should know better than to interrupt the genius at work. It's like waking a sleepwalker; could be dangerous."

Nigel crossed the room and kissed Paul, letting his hands roam over his lover's muscular body. "So what was so urgent?"

"Well," Paul said, picking lint from the front of Nigel's shirt, "if I'm going to be there by eight, I'm going to have to leave soon."

"And?" Nigel asked with a cocked eyebrow. He knew what was coming.

Paul met Nigel's eyes for a second, then looked away. "I thought I'd make one last ditch attempt to convince you to come with me."

Nigel pulled away. "Paul, how many times do we have to go through this? I have no interest in going to this little shindig of yours. I hope you have a lovely time, but I won't be joining you."

Paul had been pestering Nigel for two weeks about attending a fundraiser for the National Gay and Lesbian Task Force. Nigel was adamant about not attending, and Paul had been equally adamant on the importance of the cause. Nigel was beginning to lose patience with his lover and did not wish to have this discussion again.

"Nigel, don't you care that gays and lesbians face discrimination every day, at work and in the community? We're denied jobs, housing, physically and verbally abused; that's just the status quo."

"All the more reason to keep a low profile," Nigel said, leaving the room and heading downstairs. The maid had finished vacuuming and was now dusting the foyer. Nigel nodded at her as he passed on his way to the living room. He didn't know her name; he found it unnecessary to learn the names of the help.

"That's the wrong attitude to have," Paul was saying, following close behind Nigel. "As gay men, we need to stand up for ourselves. The world will never change as long as we stay locked up in our closets, ashamed of who we are. We need to be vocal, visible, then society will have to start recognizing us. We need to be proud of who we are."

"I am proud of who I am," Nigel said. "I'm a very rich man, and I plan to stay that way. I'm going to give you a little insight into people, free of charge. People are idiots. They are close-minded, bigoted, hypocritical, and irrational. Your radical rhetoric will never change their minds; the majority of society will always see gays as sick and demented. I cannot afford to alienate my readership. I may be in the closet, but my closet is three story, five bedroom, and two and a half bath, and that's plenty enough room for me."

"And it doesn't bother you that you're living a lie?"

"I'm a fiction writer. That's what I do, sell lies to the public."

Paul's mouth had become small and tight, a sure sign that he was enraged. His voice, instead of rising, became progressively lower. "Well, your lies have certainly worked out for you, but what about those not as fortunate? What about the sixteen-year-old who gets beat up in the locker room every day? What about the teacher who gets fired because he's considered a bad influence? What about the mother who loses her children because she just happens to be in love with another woman? What about all of them?"

"Fuck 'em," Nigel said simply, arms folded across his chest. "Who do you think I am, Mother Teresa? I can't worry about everyone in the world. I do for myself, they can take care of their own affairs."

Paul's mouth seemed to disappear and his breath exploded from his nostrils. "And what about us?" he said, voice so low it was practically inaudible.

"What about us?"

"Are you ashamed of our relationship?"

"Of course not," Nigel said a little too loudly. "But I don't see the point in advertising it, either. What we share is a private matter, not the business of the world at large. I don't care who they're fucking, why should they care who I am?"

"Am I not more to you than someone you're fucking?" Paul asked, fists clenched at his sides.

"You know you are, that's not what I'm saying. I just meant our relationship is personal, and I can think of no reason to make it public."

"I'll give you a reason. As long as you hide our relationship, you are giving de facto acquiescence."

"Speak English. I'm not impressed by your knowledge of big words."

"Your passiveness is sending a message, saying that society is right, our love is something shameful, some dark act to be kept secret. The only way gay relationships will ever be considered as valid and legitimate as straight ones is by gay couples going public, showing society that we are inherently no different than they are, that love is love."

"Cue the violins," Nigel said, running an imaginary bow across imaginary strings.

Paul closed his eyes and let a tremulous breath escape his lips. When he opened his eyes, they were wide and wet. "How can you be so callous? This is important to me. I'm not asking for much, just for you to come with me to this fundraiser."

"And I have told you a hundred times I don't want to go. Why do you insist on forcing me into this confrontation? I'm letting *you* go, isn't that enough?"

"*Letting* me go?" Paul repeated, anger roaring back into his eyes, burning up the unshed tears. "You're *letting* me go?"

"That's not what I meant," Nigel said. This argument had exhausted him, and he was ready to be done with it. "Why don't you just get out of here? You're going to be late."

"Fine. You just stay here in your selfish little shelter. Write another page, make another million, and the rest of the world can go to hell for all you care."

Paul snatched his jacket from the coat-rack and left, slamming the door behind him. The crystal chandelier above Nigel's head tinkled, creating a discordant melody. Nigel stood where he was for several minutes, unsure how things had deteriorated so quickly.

Nigel loved Paul, more than he'd ever thought he was capable of loving another. They'd met at a writer's convention in Seattle two years ago; Paul was a Ph.D. in philosophy who wrote self-help books full of New Age jargon and psychobabble. They had spent a torrid week together, which had led to Paul moving into Nigel's recently completed house. They had different viewpoints on most subjects, and arguments were as frequent as their lovemaking, but Nigel found himself depending on Paul to a degree that was frightening.

After a while, Nigel returned to his office and sat before the screen, but this time he could not find the key to open the portal.

***

"What are you saying?" Sullivan asked, staring at his maker as if at a stranger.

A pained expression twisted Delano's facial features. "I'm saying that I'm tired of hiding, tired of living in the shadows. I think we should come forward, reveal our true nature to the world."

"Are you mad? Reveal our true nature? Do you realize that would mean our deaths? We are monsters to the world; we would be hunted and destroyed."

"Maybe not," Delano persisted. "Perhaps we could find some way to peaceably coexist with the mortals."

"There is no way," Sullivan said, gripping his companion's shoulder. "Mortals will always view us as vile, evil creatures. Nothing will ever change that."

"Aren't you tired of the charade?"

"No, I am not. We mimic the mortal's ways and customs while feasting on their flesh. That has always been the way of the vampire, the night stalker. It is a life that affords us many riches without the hassles of mortal hardships."

Delano hung his head and wept.

"Take comfort, old friend," Sullivan said, holding Delano close to him. "There is much enjoyment to be squeezed from this existence. We are immortal, invincible, we have the world of darkness in our hands. Mortals are beneath us. We have no place in their world."

***

Nigel leaned back in his chair, arching his back until his spine popped. It was not quite four in the afternoon; he'd been working less than an hour. Staring at the glowing screen, Nigel felt nothing but frustration and dissatisfaction. The words weren't coming as easily today, and each sentence was a struggle to deliver from the womb of his imagination. Philip Edgers, Nigel's agent, had called this morning to check on the progress of the book; Nigel had lied and said he was halfway finished. About a third of the way through was closer to the truth. Nigel usually found the writing process to be like a faucet — once he turned the water on, there was nothing that could stop the flow until he chose to turn it off again. But something was clogging up the pipes today.

Nigel pushed away from the desk and left the room. It was rare he left the office after such a short time at work, but he needed a break. Maybe a little distance would help loosen up the block in his mind, allowing the story to flow from him freely.

As Nigel started down the hallway toward the staircase, laughter wafted up to him from downstairs. At first he thought it was only the television, but then he recognized Paul's hearty guffaw. This was followed by another, unfamiliar laugh, a high-pitched twittering. Frowning, Nigel bounded down the stairs and into the living room.

Paul was in front of the fireplace, elbow leaning casually on the mantle, a smile spread across his face like a banner. A young man, anorexic-thin, sat in Nigel's favorite recliner, wearing cut-off jeans frayed at the ends and no shirt. His emaciated torso was covered in sweat and dirt, and his damp brown hair fell over his eyes like a veil. A glass of lemonade was in his hand, and a crooked grin adorned his face. Nigel stared at this stranger for several seconds before recognizing him as the gardener.

"Oh, Greg, hi," Paul said, noticing Nigel standing mutely in the doorway. "Didn't expect you down so soon."

"Who the hell is this?" Nigel said, keeping his eyes fixed on the gardener.

"You know Bert, Greg. He tends the grounds."

"Hi there," Bert said, rising and extending a sweaty hand.

Nigel looked at the hand as if it were contaminated. "I guess I didn't recognize you since you were sitting up in here like a king and not outside working like you're supposed to be."

Bert retrieved his hand, his cheeks flushing with color, and glanced at Paul.

"Greg, don't be rude. It's over a hundred degrees outside today. I invited Bert in for a cool drink; figured it was the decent thing to do."

"Is that right?" Nigel asked, addressing the question to Bert. "You were in need of some cooling down, were you?"

"Well, it is a scorcher out there," the gardener said, shifting his weight from one foot to the other. He placed his glass on the coffee table—with no coaster, Nigel noted—and started for the archway that led into the foyer. "I guess I'll be getting back to work now. Thanks for the drink, Mr. Wells. I really appreciate it."

Paul smiled and shook the gardener's hand. "No problem, Bert. And call me Paul, please. Try not to get too hot out there. Wouldn't want you collapsing from heat exhaustion."

Bert laughed and nodded. Turning to Nigel, he said, "Nice to meet you, Mr. Nigel. I've worked here for eight months now, and I think this is the first time we've actually talked."

"Hmm, wonder what the possible reason for that could be," Nigel said, his mouth twisted in a bitter frown. "Last week you left some weeds in the azalea patch; try to do a little better today."

"Yes, sir."

After the front door closed, Nigel and Paul stood staring at one another in silence for several minutes. The air was filled with an electric tension that was tangible. Their gazes did not waver, and their eyes did not blink.

"So, you two seemed awfully chummy," Nigel said, breaking the stalemate.

"Yes, your point being?"

Nigel picked up the glass of lemonade and grunted at the ring of condensation left behind. "Oh, no point. Just seems interesting to me that you're suddenly on a first name basis with the help."

Paul rolled his eyes and sighed deeply. "I hate it when you use that word."

"Which word?"

"'Help.' Like you're the master of a plantation, and they're all your lowly servants."

"They are my lowly servants. I'm the boss, and they serve me."

"They are human beings, Greg. They work for you, yes, but they're not your indentured servants."

"No, they're *Bert*. Sitting in my chair with their greasy backs, drinking out of my crystal and staining my furniture."

"Well, God forbid. A minimum wage worker has been in this room. Let's burn everything and buy new."

"Look," Nigel said, reeling in his temper, "I don't want to argue about this. But you know how I feel about the subject. I don't want the help—sorry, the minimum wage human beings—thinking that we're their friends. Once that happens, they think they're coming here for socialization and not work. Then we'll lose our position of authority and no work will ever get done around here."

"I offered a person a cool drink on a hot day," Paul said, taking a handkerchief from his pocket and wiping away the ring from the coffee table. "I don't see how that's such a horrible crime."

"You just don't understand, Paul."

"No, I don't understand. I don't understand a bit."

Paul turned and left the room without another word. Nigel heard the bedroom door slam and Sheryl Crow begin crooning from the stereo system. That was Paul's way of saying he wanted to be alone.

"Fucking cry baby," Nigel mumbled, looking out the window at the gardener pulling weeds from the azalea patch.

***

"I don't understand why you're so upset?" Delano said, the young boy cowering behind him.

Sullivan paced the length of the crypt, nostrils flaring, fists clenched at his sides. "I'm upset because you're treating this mortal boy like he's our equal."

"I was teaching him to read, Sullivan. That's all."

"What possible need does this boy have of reading? His sole purpose is to tend to our needs and ensure we are undisturbed during our daily slumber."

Delano placed an arm around the boy's frail shoulder, pulling him close. *"He is a young man in need of an education."*

"He's our Renfield," Sullivan said, making reference to the Stoker character that served Dracula. *"He's our slave, Delano. If you treat him as an equal, he will become unruly and undisciplined. He must learn his place in the scheme of things. He is nothing more than our slave."*

"You know I am uncomfortable with the term 'slave.' Why do you insist on using it?"

Sullivan looked at his creator as he would a mentally deficient child. *"Delano, my friend, you have too much compassion for these mortals. You romanticize them. We are their superiors in every way."*

"Run along, Curt," Delano said, running a finger affectionately down the boy's cheek. After the boy disappeared up the stairs, Delano turned to Nigel and said, *"I made you, Sullivan, but I feel I don't even know you anymore."*

***

Nigel returned sooner than expected. He'd left only forty-five minutes earlier, intending to spend the afternoon at the mall, shopping his troubles away. The book was not going well. Each successive chapter was harder to finish, and what was written was lacking something, some indefinable spark that brought most of Nigel's fiction to life. In the past, it had been so simple for Nigel to slip into the mind of Sullivan, but this book felt like a pair of pants that he'd outgrown. The enjoyment was gone, dried up like a creek during a drought. Nigel had headed to the mall for a little escape.

But Nigel was not one to concede defeat. If the book was not going well, he had to *make* it go well. Running and hiding was not his style. He needed to sit in front of that word processor and not budge until he had written at least two or three chapters. The date he'd given the publisher to deliver the manuscript was fast approaching, and Nigel was barely over halfway through the novel.

After only five minutes at the mall, Nigel had gotten back in his Mustang and headed back for the house. As he pulled into the driveway, he noticed the gardener's beat-up pickup was around back, but the man himself was nowhere to be seen.

Probably having more lemonade with Paul, Nigel thought then chastised himself. Things were becoming very strained with Paul lately—which was probably the main reason he was having such a rough time writing—and Nigel did not want to go down that road. Differences they might have, but Nigel did not want to lose Paul. Paul had a way of making Nigel laugh, and he was quick to stand up for what he believed in. Even if Nigel disagreed with what Paul had to say, he had to respect his lover for having the guts to say it. Perhaps it was time for Nigel to get over himself and make a few compromises. Paul was worth it.

Nigel walked into the house and found the living room empty. The kitchen was likewise deserted. Paul's Corvette was parked in the drive so he had to be around somewhere. Faint music drifted down the stairs and Nigel followed it. Soft and forlorn, Sarah McLaughlin pining away.

Nigel paused outside the closed bedroom door, his hand trembling on the knob. So many things danced around the edges of his mind — the gardener's truck, the empty downstairs, the low sounds heard above the music — but Nigel pushed them aside, not wanting to look at them directly.

Pushing open the door, Nigel looked on the scene with numb dispassion. Paul was lying on his back, hands resting behind his head. The gardener sat atop him, straddling him, rocking his hips and moaning softly. Paul thrust his pelvis upward, eliciting a hiss from the gardener, and murmured, "Yes, oh yes, Bert, you feel so good."

"What is this?" Nigel said softly, but then the numbness dissipated like smoke, leaving a fiery rage in its wake. "What the fuck is this?" he shouted.

The gardener yelped and rolled off of Paul, grabbing the sheets to cover his nakedness. Paul bolted up against the headboard, eyes wide and mouth slack, an idiot savant caught doing something naughty.

Hot tears rolled down Nigel's cheeks, and his chest heaved as if about to explode. He walked further into the room, seeing the clothes strewn about, the opened bottle of lube on the nightstand, the condom wrappers littering the floor. Two condom wrappers.

"Greg," Paul said in a breathy whisper, grabbing his boxers from one of the bedposts and slipping them on. His erection shriveled like a slug sprinkled with salt. "My God, Greg, I, we, oh god."

"How long?" Nigel asked. Everything had a surreal quality to it, the colors a little too bright, the angles slightly skewed, and his skin felt too tight for the skeleton it covered. He expected any moment for his insides to tear through the outer shell.

The gardener had grabbed a handful of his clothes and made a break for the hallway, but Nigel kicked the door closed with his foot.

"Don't leave yet, Bert. We've got things to discuss here."

The young man cringed into the corner, crying, snot running from his nose. He wiped at it with the back of his arm and slid down the wall, squatting with his knees to his chin.

"Greg, I'm sorry," Paul said, approaching Nigel with upheld hands. "I didn't mean for you to find out this way."

Nigel squeezed his eyes shut and put his hands to his head, as if trying to keep his brain from popping out of his skull. He grabbed a Dalmatian-shaped figurine from the dresser and slung it across the room, where it shattered against the far wall. Black-and-white shards rained down on the gardener's head.

"I am truly sorry," Paul said, reaching out a hand to Nigel. "I was going to tell you soon, I swear."

With an apocalyptic roar, Nigel lashed out, delivering a hard jab to Paul's nose. Paul fell back onto the bed, a thin line of blood dribbling from his left nostril. He looked dazed.

"Get out," Nigel said in a hiss. "You and your little slut. Get the fuck out of my house this minute. Don't bother to pack, you can send for your stuff. I don't want to look at your face for a second more. I won't be held responsible for my actions if I have to."

Paul motioned with his head, and the gardener rushed past Nigel and out the door. Nigel could hear him clomping down the stairs and out the front door, his clothes still in his arms. Paul took his pants from the floor and put them on. He took his time finding his shirt and shoes.

Nigel sank into the chair at the vanity table, all the strength leaking from his body and leaving him weak and shaking. "Why?" he said in a croak.

"It wasn't just some frivolous fling," Paul said, sitting on the bed and tying his shoes. "I know that doesn't help, but it wasn't just sex. I've fallen in love with Bert."

"I thought you were in love with me." Nigel flinched at the pathetic whining quality of his own voice.

"I do love you," Paul said, staring at his shoes. "But we don't fit, Nigel. We have nothing in common, and we obviously see the world in very different ways. It would never work between us."

"But it will work between you and that dirt-digging nitwit?"

"Bert is a very intelligent man; he's just had some tough breaks in life. But he's taking night classes to get his C.N.A. After that, he wants to go to college for nursing."

"And you think I give a shit about his ambitions?"

Paul lifted his eyes and met Nigel's gaze. Paul's eyes were red and brimming with unshed tears. "Bert and I are better suited. His temperament matches my own, and we want the same things out of life. I'm sorry that I hurt you, but this has been coming long before Bert entered the picture."

"Get out. Just get out before I punch you again."

Paul hesitated, opened his mouth but then shook his head without speaking. He walked to the door, head down, and paused in the doorway. "Goodbye, Greg," he said, then left.

Nigel sat at the vanity for some time, listening as the Corvette cranked and roared down the drive. Nigel looked at himself in the mirror, the blubbering mess that he had become. Love had made him weak, vulnerable, opened him up for this. He was disgusted with himself. He slammed his fist into the mirror, splintering the glass and opening up several gashes in his knuckles. He did not even feel the pain.

Nigel did not move. He sat with his bloody hand in his lap and refused to cry.

***

When Sullivan entered the crypt, he found the Renfield on his knees, sucking hungrily at the wound in Delano's wrist. Delano stood, head back, eyes closed, an orgasmic smile on his lips.

"Delano, what are you doing?"

The Renfield pulled away, his lips bloodied, his eyes glassy. Nigel could see he was too late. The change had already been enacted; Delano's preternatural blood had forever altered the boy, snatching him from the world of the mortal and delivering him into the world of the immortal.

Delano came around slowly, and he stared at Sullivan for several moments before recognition sparked in his eyes. "Sullivan, dear boy, back so soon?"

"You made this boy one of us?" Sullivan said, incredulity dripping from his words. "You imparted the magic to him?"

"You can see quite plainly that I have."

"But why? He will only slow us down; we will have to take the time to teach him the ways and customs of the night stalker."

Delano laughed, and the sound was cold and empty. "You need not worry about that, Sullivan."

"And why is that?"

"Because the boy is my new companion. Think of him as your replacement."

Sullivan could not speak, could not comprehend what he was hearing.

"Yes," Delano continued, taking the boy by the hand. "I need someone who thinks like I, whose needs match my own. That is not you. Curt, on the other hand, he is what I need."

"How can you say these things?"

"You are a monster," Delano said with a sneer. "So much more than I ever was or ever could be. And I think I have finally figured out why. You were a monster before I ever gave you the gift. The vampiric blood only intensified it."

"This can't be. You prefer this mere boy over me." Sullivan punched a fist through the cement wall of the crypt, crumbling the rock and splitting open the skin of his hand. Sullivan dropped to the floor.

Delano encouraged the boy to leave them, and the Renfield hurried past Sullivan and up the steps to the waiting night. "I apologize," Delano said, offering Sullivan a melancholy smile. "I wish there was some other way, but this is how it must be."

Without awaiting a response, Delano left the crypt, leaving Sullivan alone with the dead.

Sullivan did not move. He sat with his bloody hand in his lap and refused to cry.

THE END

***

THE END

A local radio station actually did a similar thing every December, and I would listen, wondering what would happen if they pulled this stunt on a family that didn't want people rummaging around in their house…

Breaking-and-Entering Christmas

Transcript from the December 22nd broadcast of the Dillard and Kimbo morning show on radio station WJAM.

Dillard: Hi folks. For those of you just tuning in, Kimbo and I are broadcasting live on remote today for our annual Breaking-and-Entering Christmas event. Longtime fans of the show will know what this is all about.

Kimbo: If you're new to the radio family, every year starting around Thanksgiving, we have listeners nominate needy families in the area that could use a little Christmas miracle. We select one family, then the week leading up to Christmas while everyone in the household is out, we have a friend or relative let us into the home and we put up a tree and decorations and leave mounds of presents.

Dillard: Here comes Santa Claus. Ho! Ho! Ho!

Kimbo: Hey, who you calling a ho?

Dillard: Well, if the stocking fits...

Kimbo: Watch it there, Dillard, you may get a lump of coal upside the head. Anyway, the lucky family chosen for this year's Breaking-and-Entering Christmas is the Grahams. Patricia and Pete and their three kids—9 year old Kristy, 12 year old Randy, and 14 year old Buck. And with us today is Pete's cousin Tony, the one who nominated the family.

Tony: Pete and his family are good folks, just been a bit down on their luck lately is all. The plant where both Pete and Patty worked went outta business, and what with the economy the way it is, they ain't been able to find work nowhere else. The unemployment checks don't cover much, and the kids ain't had no new clothes or toys in almost a year. I hate seeing 'em suffer like they do, and I help out all I can, but that ain't much.

Dillard: You said in your letter to us that they didn't even have a tree.

Tony: Nope, they said they was just gonna ignore Christmas this year, they couldn't afford to celebrate. Tell ya, that's the saddest damn thing I ever heard.

Kimbo: You don't have to be sad anymore. We're going to bring some holiday cheer into their lives.

Dillard: You're sure they'll be out for a while, right?

Tony: Oh yeah. The kids are at their Grandma's, and Pete and Patty went to the unemployment office. We should have a few hours, for definite.

Dillard: Good, because here we are.

Sounds of car doors opening and closing, scuffling and slapping of feet on pavement.

Kimbo: We're outside the house now, a little single-story Ranch style. Looks kind of sad with its peeling paint and missing shutters.

Dillard: Also, it's the only house on the block that's not decorated. No lights, no reindeer lawn ornaments, not even a wreath on the door.

Tony: Told ya, they ain't doing Christmas this year. Pete says he's got some prospects for making some quick cash so maybe they can do a late Christmas after the New Year, but I know my cuz. His "quick cash" schemes never amount to a hill of beans.

Dillard: Well, we can certainly give the family a good holiday. We have the van loaded up with a tree, ornaments, stockings, fruits and candies, a 12 pound Turkey for Christmas dinner, and that doesn't even include all the presents.

Kimbo: For Patricia, we have makeup, hair care products, perfume, shoes. We're loading Pete up with an expensive tool kit, an electric razor, and a gun rack since Tony tells us he's an avid hunter. And the kids are getting a variety of clothes and school supplies, as well as dolls, stuffed animals, and a tea-set for Kristy and action figures, model cars, and CDs for the boys. And for the entire family, a Wii game system with a collection of a dozen games.

Dillard: I can only imagine how overjoyed the family is going to be when they get home tonight and find all this waiting for them.

Kimbo: So Tony, you ready to let us in?

Tony: Oh yeah.

A scrape, a clattering, then the sound of a lock disengaging.

Tony: They always keep an extra key under the flowerpot on the front porch.

Kimbo: *(laughing)* Well, they'll have to come up with a different hiding place for it now that all our listeners know about this one.

Dillard: Otherwise the tens of fifteens of people who tune in might try to break in after us.

Kimbo: Oh Dillard, our numbers have gone up a lot lately. Last ratings I saw, we had at least twenty listeners who — *Oh my God!*

Coughing and gagging noises in the background.

Dillard: Man, it reeks in here. Jesus, look at all this crap. It's a pigsty in here.

Tony: I haven't been over in a while, I had no idea — (*a pause and a retching sound*) — I didn't know it was this bad.

Dillard: It's like a trash dump. Garbage everywhere, dirty dishes covered in mold all over the floor, pizza boxes and take-out containers. It's hard to even find any bare floor to put your foot down, the place is just carpeted in filth. I've seen landfills that were neater than this.

Kimbo: I guess this just shows how far they've fallen on hard times.

Dillard: Hell, they're both out of work, you'd think they'd have plenty of time for housekeeping.

Kimbo: Have a little compassion. When you're down on your luck, it's easy to sink into a depression that leaves you without the energy to even do the simplest tasks. That's the way it was for me after my second divorce. People shouldn't have to live this way. I guess as part of our gift-giving this year we'll also do a little cleaning for them.

Dillard: Are you out of your mind? I don't even think we should be in here without Haz-Mat suits.

Tony: I'm with the Dill-Man on this one. I love my cuz and all, but this place is gross with a capital YUCK!

Kimbo: Well, at least let's clear some room to put up the tree.

Dillard: Oh man, got a shovel.

Tony: Why don't we just pull the couch away from the wall there and shove it in the corner? That'll clear some space by the window for the tree.

Dillard: Let's get it over with and get the hell out of here before I puke.

Kimbo: Dillard, let's not forget this is a charitable thing we're doing here.

Dillard: Staying in this mess a second longer than necessary goes beyond simple charity. Now let's get to work.

Grunting and the sound of something scraping along the floor, some soft cursing.

Tony: This is a heavy sumbitch.

Kimbo: Watch the language, Tony; remember we're on the air.

Dillard: Christ, there's more trash under the couch. I can't believe — wait a minute, is that...?

Kimbo: What is that? Bags of flour?

Dillard: Uhm, I don't think so. I think we should go now.

Tony: Holy hell, that's cocaine, ain't it?

Dillard: We need to go.

Kimbo: I think you're right.

Tony: Christ man, this must be how Pete's planning to make that quick cash. I didn't have a clue he was into this shit, I swear.

Dillard: We can talk about it in the van, let's just —

Sound of a door bursting open.

Unidentified male voice: What's this happy horseshit? Just who are you people and what in the name of fuck ya'll doing in our house?

Tony: Pete, man, chill, it's me.

Unidentified male voice: Tony, what the Sam Hell you doing here, and who're these douche bags you got with you?

Unidentified female voice: Christ on a cracker, they done found our stash, Pete.

Unidentified male voice: You trying to rip us off, Tony? That it?

Dillard: Let's just calm down, folks. I can explain. We're with a radio station, WJAM, and Tony here entered you in this contest —

Unidentified female voice: Get away from the stash, bitch!

A loud smack, and the sound of a woman screaming, possibly Kimbo.

Unidentified male voice: That does it! Cousin or not, I ain't gonna let you rip me off, Tony.

Tony: It's not like that, I swear.

Dillard: Jesus, put the gun down, man. Just hear me out.

Kimbo: *(crying)* Oh God, help us.

Unidentified female voice: Shut the fuck up.

A meaty wack, the sound of someone woofing out breath, then something heavy hitting the floor.

Unidentified male voice: Merry fucking Christmas everybody! Santa's about to deliver some buckshot right into your sorry thieving asses.

Tony: No man, wait!

Dillard: Don't do it!

Kimbo: (*Unintelligible sobbing.*)

Unidentified female voice: Let 'em have it, Pete. No mercy.

The roar of gunfire, screaming and cursing, shattering glass, heavy thuds, then nothing but dead air...

This one was written to try to get into an anthology but unfortunately didn't make the cut. I think the editor wanted stories more supernaturally based, but I do find this one rather disturbing and am proud of it.

What Little Boys are Made of

When Barry didn't find Eric in his room, he knew exactly where his son must be. Stalking down the hall, he opened the door to the attic stairwell. He resisted the urge to pound up the steps yelling the boy's name. Better to sneak up and catch Eric in the act.

As Barry crept slowly up the stairs, he could hear his son in the attic, mumbling in a high-pitched, squeaky voice. He felt his anger rise like a helium balloon, but he caught hold of the string before it could soar out of his reach. The boy would have to be disciplined again, but last time Barry had gotten a bit carried away and he'd ended up having to take Eric to the emergency room to treat a dislocated shoulder. The ER staff seemed to have bought the story about Eric taking a tumble off a jungle gym at the park, but Barry couldn't risk any more trips to the hospital; it would only arouse suspicion. And how Barry raised his son was nobody else's goddamn business no matter how much society seemed to believe it was, which was one of the main reasons he was homeschooling the boy. People always wanted to put their noses where they didn't belong, interfering in personal family matters.

Barry stepped up into the shadowy attic. There was only a single bulb in the center of the ceiling but it was not lit; the string you pulled to turn it on was not long enough for eight-year-old Eric to reach. Still, there was a large circular window at the far end of the open attic space through which copious amounts of late afternoon sunlight poured in, creating a spotlight effect on the boy. Eric was sitting with his back to the staircase, seemingly oblivious to his father's presence, doing exactly what Barry had feared.

Playing with those damn dolls.

"BOY!" Barry suddenly roared, his voice filling the attic like the thunderous bellow of God himself.

Eric didn't jump or squeal in surprise. He merely stiffened, almost as if he'd been expecting to be caught. He turned slowly toward his father, still holding one of the dolls in his hand. He didn't even have the sense to drop it. "Hello, sir."

"Is that all you can say to me? Just what in the hell are you doing up in the attic?"

The boy gave a weary shrug, moving as if he had anvils resting on his shoulders. "I was just playing."

Barry crossed the distance between them in four long strides, snatching the doll from Eric's grasp. A vintage Barbie, Disco Barbie it looked like judging from the outfit. Glancing down, Barry saw that the trunk was open and at least a dozen Barbie's had been taken out and arranged around the wooden floor.

These dolls had belonged to Melinda, Barry's late wife. He should have thrown them out after Melinda was killed in that car accident three years ago, but he had kept them for sentimental reasons, storing them up here in the attic. But now that Eric couldn't stay away from them, he was thinking throwing them out might be his only option. One of those touchy-feely therapists might say that the boy was drawn to the dolls because they represented the mother he could barely remember, but by God, no son of Barry's was going to grow up all faggy. It was his job to teach Eric how to be a real man, and real men didn't play with goddamn dolls!

"How many times have we been over this?" he growled at the boy. "You have plenty of toys downstairs, why do you insist on sneaking up here to play with these?"

Another of those anvil shrugs. "I don't know, I just like them I guess."

Barry lashed out and struck Eric across the cheek with Disco Barbie. "That's no kind of answer. So the toys I buy for you aren't good enough, is that what you're saying?"

"N-no, sir."

"You have remote control cars, army men, toy guns, a whole selection of video games. Those are toys for boys. These stupid Barbies are for girls. Are you a girl?"

Eric mutely shook his head.

Barry dropped to his knees and grabbed his son by the neck, yanking him close until their noses were almost touching in an Eskimo kiss. "Don't shake your head at me, speak! I said, are you a girl?"

"No, sir. I'm a b-boy."

"Then start acting like it," Barry spat, shoving the boy over onto his back where his head connected with the floor with a hollow *thunk*. "And don't you start crying, either. A man endures pain without blubbering like a bitch."

Eric scrambled to his feet, wiping at his eyes before the tears could fall. "Yes, sir."

Barry began gathering up the dolls and tossing them back in the trunk. "I cannot believe you are doing this to me. All I've ever wanted is a son, and after your mother and I had you, I had the misfortune of getting testicular cancer and now I can't have any more kids, so you're my only shot. And what do I end up with? A damn sissy."

"I'm not a sissy, sir."

"Really? Could have fooled me. Only girls and sissies play with dolls. You get on downstairs and wait for your punishment."

"But sir—"

"Don't question me!" Barry roared, backhanding the boy and sending him to the floor again. "You do what I say when I say. Now move your—"

Barry paused abruptly as he picked up yet another doll off the floor and got a good look at it. Obviously a Barbie with those delicate features and impossible curves, but this one had been altered. Presumably by Eric. The hair had been hacked off rather crudely into some kind of military buzz, and whatever outfit she had originally worn had been replaced by some clothes from Ken's wardrobe. Cross-dressing Barbie, maybe.

"Get downstairs," Barry said again, but this time his voice was quieter, not so heated. Eric made for the stairs but paused when his father called his name again. "And you shouldn't be running around without your socks."

Eric nodded then hurried downstairs.

***

Eric paced around his room, waiting for his father, terrified of the punishment that was to be doled out. Absently, the boy rubbed at his shoulder, remembering the pain of having it dislocated. Maybe if he cleaned his room while he waited, that would appease some of his father's anger.

The boy began gathering up his toys and taking them to the closet, not just dumping them but arranging them neatly. He glanced at all the clothes hanging on the rod. Boring clothes, not like the colorful dresses that he dimly remembered getting to wear back before Mother had died, back when his name had still been Erica.

Staring down at his feet, Eric remembered his father's last admonishing in the attic about running around without his socks. Didn't want to make the old man even more irate. Eric hurried over to the dresser and pulled out a balled-up pair of socks.

Then stuffed them down his pants.

Everyone parent's worst nightmare has to be that something terrible will happen to their children. How much worse is the fear that the parent could be the one responsible…

Parental Instincts

Jerry looked down at his three-month old daughter sleeping in the crib and thought, *I could kill her.*

The thought was so alien that it actually startled him, causing him to jerk upright and look around the room as if the voice had come from somewhere other than his own head. Why would he think such a thing? He loved May, she was his world.

I'm not saying I would kill her, just that I could.

Jerry shook his head as if he could dislodge these horrible thoughts. Where were they coming from? He could never hurt May.

Sure I could. It would be easy. She's so small and defenseless. There are dozens of ways I could do it.

Shaken, Jerry stumbled out of the nursery and leaned against the hallway wall. Sleep depravation, that was the cause of this. Lack of sleep and grief. Since Julie had died from complications giving birth to May, Jerry had been left to raise the baby alone. She kept him up most nights, and he hadn't had more than a few hours sleep at a time in months.

Think how much better my life would be if I just killed her. I could sleep nights, go out whenever I wanted. I'd have my life back.

"Stop it!" Jerry shouted out loud. This awakened May and she started crying, a high-pitched wail that sounded to Jerry's ears like a banshee shrieking.

I could put a pillow over her face, then I'd never have to hear that wail again.

Instead of going to May to comfort her, Jerry shuffled down the hall into the living room, dropping to his knees by the sofa and placing his hands over his ears. It didn't even begin to block out May's screams. What was wrong with him? Was he going insane?

Yes, and it's all May's fault. That little bitch is driving me nuts with her neediness and dependence.

Jerry began pulling at his hair, as if maybe he could dig these thoughts out of his mind. How could he even consider such things? May was precious to him; she was all he had left of Julie.

A baby belongs with its mother. Since Julie's in heaven, that's where I should send May.

May was still screaming, the cries carrying down the hall, seeking Jerry out and battering him with their insistent need. He wanted to go to her, but he was afraid. He didn't trust himself at the moment. The voice in his head, it wasn't a stranger's voice whispering these unspeakable things; it was his own.

You'd think that bitch would have tired herself out with all that yowling. What does she have to cry about anyway? I take care of her every goddamn whim. She's screaming like somebody's trying to kill her. Maybe somebody should.

"Oh Jesus," Jerry groaned, biting down on his tongue, hoping the pain would give him clarity of mind. The thoughts were starting to sound less alien to him, starting to make too much sense. That scared him more than anything.

Julie was the one who wanted a kid in the first fucking place. Then she goes and sticks me with it all by myself. I didn't sign up to be a single dad.

"I won't, I won't, I won't," Jerry began saying, repeating the two words like a mantra. He was a good man; he wasn't a murderer.

She's three months old, that's barely a person. It wouldn't really be murder. More like abortion, only a little later in the game than usual.

Jerry was shocked to find himself on his feet and heading toward the hallway, toward the nursery. It took a great deal of effort to halt his progress and retreat back toward the sofa.

The sooner I get this over with, the better. That baby is a chain around my neck, an albatross like in that story I read in Freshman English. It's time I freed myself from this burden.

Jerry could feel himself weakening again, could feel the pull of that voice leading him toward the nursery, toward an act for which he would never be able to forgive himself. He reached for the phone. He was a danger to himself and his daughter; he had to get help. He punched in the three numbers, having to force himself not to hang up.

"911, what is the nature of your emergency?"

"Yes, please," he said, the words coming out as a sob. "It's my daughter."

"Is she hurt?"

"She's only three months old. I went in to check on her and…and…"

"Sir? What's wrong with your daughter?"

"She isn't breathing. I think she's dead."

Atta boy. Knew I could do it.

Even as he recited his address, he was reaching for one of the sofa's throw pillows.

This is one of my favorite of my flash pieces. The plot itself isn't all that original, but I like the structure of the story very much, and I think it tells a familiar tale in an interesting way. And incidentally, the criticism "you write like you watch too much TV" is something I was told in a rejection letter once.

Won't Take No for an Answer

Hayden Templeton   approx.543 words
153 Goldenrod Terrance, Apt. 2F
Paynesville, SC
htempleton@coolmail.com

WON'T TAKE NO FOR AN ANSWER
by Hayden Templeton

Larry Yablans was tied to a chair in his home office, duct tape covering his mouth to keep him from screaming. Tears had left slug trails down the sides of his face, and his eyes remained wide as he stared across the room at Harris Thompson, his captor.

"You brought this on yourself," Harris said, pacing the room. "I mean, there's only so much a man can take, and you pushed me to the edge then over. I really had no choice, you left me no choice."

Larry tried to speak, but all that came out was a garbled, muffled mumbling. He tried to work the tape loose with his tongue, but it was wound several times all the way around his head.

"Fifteen stories," Harris said, squatting down in front of Larry so that the two men were eye to eye. "I submitted fifteen stories to your publication, and you rejected every single one of them."

Larry tried to move his hands, but his wrists were securely tied to the arms of the chair, making even the slightest movement impossible. He started to cry again, fresh tears following the dried tracks down his cheeks.

Harris waved a stack of crinkled papers in Larry's face. "Some of the stories you rejected were published in other magazines, so I know they're good. What, do you have some kind of vendetta against me? Maybe you're jealous of my talent. Is that it? I mean, if you had any real talent you'd be out publishing your own stuff instead of playing editor at some second-rate flash fiction mag."

Here Harris paused while he riffled through the papers. "You started out just sending typical form rejections. 'Your piece has merit but just isn't right for us', 'We regret to inform you we are passing on your story but try us again with something else.' But then you started sending personal rejections. This one for my story 'Piece of Garbage' says that my characters are one dimensional and without distinction; the one for 'Habitat for Inhumanity' says I have no sense of pacing and the ending is too implausible. You called my story 'Harvest Night' a string of clichés and unoriginal ideas. And here, in your rejection of 'Bitten by the Bug', you say I write like I watch too much TV, whatever the hell that means."

Larry continued to struggle against his bonds, even though he knew it was pretty much hopeless. Still, he had to try. His wife and seven-year-old son were somewhere in the house; there was no telling what this loon had done to them.

"Fifteen rejections," Harris was saying softly, as if talking to himself. "Fifteen perfectly good stories just tossed aside by you. I couldn't let that pass, couldn't let that go unpunished."

Harris stood and walked behind the chair, out of Larry's line of sight. Larry didn't like not knowing where Harris was or what he was doing.

Larry smelled the gas before he felt it splash over his head. The fumes were overwhelmingly strong, and Larry began bucking in the chair that had become his prison as if he were riding a bronco.

Harris walked back around the chair so that Larry could see him as he lit the match.

***

Lawrence Youngblood
Flash in the Pan Magazine
Payton, West Virginia

November 4, 2008

Hayden Templeton
153 Goldenrod Terrance, Apt. 2F
Paynesville, SC

Dear Mr. Templeton:

I will not be accepting your story "Won't Take No for an Answer" for publication in *Flash in the Pan*. The successful piece of flash fiction manages to create fully realized characters and a complete, satisfying story in a thousand words or less, and your story does not manage to do this. Larry and Harris are the merest suggestions of characters with nothing that makes them stand out as real individuals, and the story itself raises more questions than it answers. The hook of the story—unbalanced writer seeking revenge—has been done before and much better.

I know you have been submitting stories regularly here for the past year, but I want to give you a bit of advice. Before you send me anything else of yours, pause to consider if writing is really something about which you are passionate. Perhaps your energies would be best directed elsewhere.

Sincerely,
Lawrence Youngblood

***

Hayden stood just inside the door, the shredded envelope on the floor at his feet. He'd read the rejection letter a dozen times and read it once more for good measure. The last paragraph especially got to him, like a kick to the balls. The editor was practically telling Hayden "don't quit your day job."

Moving on numb legs, Hayden walked through the house, leaving the front door open, to his little office space in the back. He dropped heavily into the folding chair at his desk, the laptop before him. He opened up the center drawer and placed the letter with the other rejections he'd received from *Flash in the Pan*. Fourteen other rejections.

Closing the drawer, he turned his attention to his computer and pulled up Internet Explorer. There was a search engine link on his toolbar, and he typed in the name "Lawrence Youngblood" and hit Enter.

The Internet was an amazing thing; there was nothing you couldn't find out about a person. Including his home address.

I have a fondness for this one even though it isn't much of a story, more a vignette, a strange conversation. I love the voice of the main character though, and her non-logic that is both sweet and tragic.

What's Done's Done

"What is your name?"

She looked up at the officer from underneath her veil of chestnut brown bangs. One shoulder lifted in a nearly imperceptible shrug. "Don't got one."

"Everyone has a name."

"Gave mine away a long time ago. Don't remember what it was, but it don't matter. Ain't mine no more."

"So what do your friends call you?"

A pained expression crossed her face but she said nothing.

"Don't have any friends?"

A slight shake of her head was her only answer.

"Family?"

"Gave them away with my name. Sort of a package deal." She laughed at this, the sound ringing hollow in the small room.

"Where did you meet Vick Boyd?"

"Around. He was nice to me. Asked me back to his place a lot. Always offered me money."

"So he was your regular john?"

Her eyes flashed hot and angry. "I said he offered me money, but I never said I took it. I did him for free."

"Awfully generous of you."

"Like I said, he was nice to me."

"Then why'd you kill him?"

She fidgeted in her seat, picking at a scab on her forearm that was already dribbling blood. "He tried to take something from me."

"I thought you were giving it away."

"Not *that*. He coulda had that, but he wanted something else."

"Such as?"

"This." She pointed at her chest.

"I thought those were part of what you were giving him. A package deal, as you said."

She rolled her eyes. "I'm talking about my heart. He wanted my heart."

"I'm not following."

"He said I was special and he wanted me off the streets. He said I could move in with him, and he'd take care of me."

"Very nice offer."

"I told you he was nice."

"And that's why you killed him?"

"I killed him because he wanted my heart. He wanted to know my name, he wanted to know *me*."

"And you couldn't allow that?"

"There's no me to know, but he wouldn't accept that. Kept pushing, 'til finally I had to push back."

"That's when you stabbed him?"

"He was trying to take my heart. I had to stop him. It's was whatchacallit...self defense."

"So you feel justified in your actions?"

She seemed uncertain for a moment, lost. Her eyes darted around the room before landing back on the officer. "I'd rather it not have happened, but what's done's done."

"I have just one more question for you. After you killed him, why did you call the police and then wait around for them to arrive? Why not just leave the body behind and get the hell out of dodge?"

She shrugged again, a child's gesture. "Because he was nice to me."

This story may frustrate some because of its ambiguity, but that's precisely why I like it. There's something to be said for a story that doesn't spell everything out for readers, leaving them to draw their own conclusions. This was originally published by Flash Me Magazine *in 2008.*

A Midnight Errand

He kneels down by the edge of the water. The moon reflects on the still surface, as if it has been captured and chained in the depths of the pond. He holds a towel-wrapped bundle against his chest; red stains seep through the towel and mar his white shirt, but he pays this no heed. He merely kneels there, swaying slightly like a weed in a breeze though the night air holds its breath, staring at the moon's mirror image in the water as if expecting it to rise up and return to its rightful place in the heavens.

There are tear tracks on his cheeks, but they are old and dry now. What he feels cannot accurately be labeled as grief. In fact, he doesn't really feel anything at all. Just a numbness, a hollowness in the center of his being. As if his insides have all been scooped out and now he's just an empty shell that hasn't yet caved in on itself. But will given time.

He can hear the sounds of cars on the highway a few miles away. And when he looks out across the pond, he can even see the headlights spearing through the darkness. But that is like another world, a distant star that has no bearing on his own existence. The people manning those faraway cars are not even the same species as he is. They simply can't be.

Looking down at the bundle in his arms, he notices the red smears on his shirt. Like little roses blossoming on the fabric. His chest has become a garden, his soul the verdant soil in which the flowers take root. What a poetic notion, as most lies are.

His wife waits for him somewhere in the night, in a place called "home," though the word no longer holds much meaning for him. He should finish this task quickly and return to her, he knows he should, and yet he remains where he is, cradling the bundle. Wrapped up the way it is, the thing is shapeless, could be anything. It could be a football or a small watermelon swaddled in the towel, if not for the red stains.

For a brief instant, he thinks he hears his wife calling his name, but that is of course absurd. She is nowhere near the pond. She is at "home," in that other world of which he no longer feels a part. She is waiting for him, and she is not a patient woman.

Finally, he lowers the bundle, pushing it beneath the surface of the pond, creating ripples in the water that make the moon waver like a mirage. Still he does not release the bundle, holding onto it for a moment more. The hollowness inside him fills up with an intense aching, but only for a moment and then he is emptied out again. He releases the bundle and lets it sink.

As the bundle descends slowly into the depths to join the moon in its watery prison, he thinks for a moment that he sees something struggling weakly inside the towel, but surely that is only his imagination.

A nasty little Halloween tale that was originally set to appear in the re-release of my collection Dark Treats. *The publisher decided not to add any additional stories however. I rather enjoy the piece, and offer it to you now.*

Prank

"I don't think we should be out here," Jessica said, a tremor in her voice.

Brent laughed in the darkness. "You're not scared, are you?"

"Of course I'm scared. I'm wandering around in a graveyard on Halloween night. Any sane person would be scared. Actually, any sane person would be back in her dorm room studying for her Bio exam."

"Come on, Jess, this is romantic."

"Um, no it isn't. Romantic is a candlelit dinner at a swanky restaurant; romantic is bringing me flowers for no particular reason; romantic is meeting me outside class just because you want to see me. Dragging me through a cemetery after dark is not romantic."

"It's Halloween," Brent said, putting his arm around her waist and pulling her close to him. "We're supposed to be doing spooky stuff like this."

"Correction, *kids* are supposed to do stuff like this. We're college students, we should be a little more grown-up, don't you think?"

"But we're only freshman, I think we still have some juvenile tendencies to work out."

"You don't fool me for a second," Jessica said with a giggle. "You just want to do it outdoors. You're such a little freak."

"And that's what you love about me, am I right?"

"Well, I don't—"

Suddenly a figure in dark clothes and a black ski-mask bolted out from behind a large monument and grabbed Jessica around the waist, throwing her to the ground. She screamed and tried to crawl away, but the guy was on top of her, holding her down with his weight as he tugged at her sweater. She flailed out, trying to knock him off of her, but he was too strong.

Then Brent was there, wrapping a muscled arm around the guy's neck and yanking him back. "What the fuck?" her attacker muttered, but then Brent twisted viciously and there was a loud *crack* and the guy fell to the ground like a sack of bricks.

"Are you okay?" Brent said, kneeling next to Jessica. "Did that creep hurt you?"

She shook her head. "I'm okay, but is he…?"

Cautiously, Brent approached the prone form of the attacker, reaching out and checking his wrist for a pulse. "Christ, I think I might have killed him. I didn't mean to, I was just trying to get him off you."

"Who is it?"

The guy was lying on his stomach, and with a grunt of effort Brent rolled him over then lifted up the ski mask. Both he and Jessica gasped aloud.

"Shit, isn't that your roommate?" Jessica asked.

"Yeah, it's Kenny."

"What in the name of God was he doing?"

Brent flopped hard onto his backside, rocking back and forth like a child. "I told him I was planning to bring you out here tonight. He must have decided to play a Halloween prank on us. Oh fuck, I...I..."

There were no more words as Brent broke into sobs, burying in face in his hands. Jessica knelt next to him and took him into her arms, allowing him to cry on her shoulder. "Shh, it's okay, you couldn't have known."

One day prior...

Brent and Kenny lay in bed together, Kenny nestled up to his roommate's side. The room stank of sex and their bodies were slicked with a glistening sheen of sweat. Brent glanced at the clock and said, "I need to go shower; I'm meeting Jessica at the Student Center at eight."

He felt Kenny stiffen next to him. "Do you have to go?"

"You know the answer to that one. Jessica is my girlfriend."

"Your beard is more like it."

Brent sighed, sitting up and throwing his feet onto the floor. "Do we have to get into this again?"

"I just don't understand why you have to pretend with her when everything is so right between us."

"I told you, I have a certain reputation to maintain. I'm captain of the lacrosse team, president of the campus Young Republicans, and my father is a Baptist minister for fuck's sake. I can't very well tell the world that I'm a flaming faggot."

"Why not?" Kenny said, propping himself up on an elbow. "I mean, it's better than living a lie."

Brent glanced over his shoulder, shooting Kenny a withering glare. "Look, when we're alone in this room we can do whatever we want, but outside these walls I have a certain image I want to maintain, and it doesn't include being a fudge-packer. Jessica helps me maintain that image."

"It's going to come out sooner or later."

Brent got very quiet for a moment, and his stare became lethal. "Are you threatening me?"

Kenny shrank under the covers. "No."

"Well, only the two of us know about this, so it's not going to come out unless one of us runs our fucking mouths. And that's not going to happen, right?"

Kenny didn't answer.

"Right?" Brent said louder.

Kenny nodded. "I guess not."

Brent stood, striding naked across the room to his closet. He stood there motionless for several minutes, feeling his roommate's stare on his back. Finally he took a deep breath and turned around. "Kenny, I know this might be a bad time, but I want to ask a favor of you?"

Kenny sat up, his eager-to-please expression making him look like a puppy that is always happy to see its master no matter how many times it gets kicked. "You know I'd do anything for you."

Brent flashed his most charming smile. "Want to help me play a little Halloween prank on Jessica tomorrow night?"

I will interject here to say I have been criticized in the past for writing stories that feature unscrupulous and sometimes downright villainous gay characters. The way I see it is thusly, writers utilize straight villains all the time and don't take flak for it. Gay people can be hero or villain, just like straight people. That's real equality, not being seen as better or less-than but just the same.

Making Ends Meet

Russ didn't know why he'd come to the circus. He'd always hated the circus, even when he was a small child. It was the clowns, with their grotesque greasepaint smiles and sinister laughter. He knew it was a cliché, being afraid of clowns, but that did nothing to allay the sense of dread he felt when he saw them piling out of their tiny little cars. When he looked at them all he saw was John Wayne Gacy, Pennywise, Ronald McDonald, who Russ had always thought had a whiff of child molester in those old McDonald's commercials from his childhood.

So why had he come to the circus alone now? He hadn't even brought Becca along with him, but she was seven months pregnant and often didn't feel like going out anywhere.

There wasn't much of a crowd in the Big Top. Maybe twenty people in the circular stands that looked down on the center ring, kind of a paltry turnout. Russ sat near the very top of the stands in a nearly deserted section. Below, the Ringmaster introduced the next act, which was a lion tamer. Russ was surprised to find a bag of popcorn in his hands; he didn't even remember buying it. He tossed a few kernels in his mouth as he watched the performer wielding a chair and a whip, keeping the ferocious beast at bay. Russ liked this kind of act, the thrill of danger that didn't touch him personally.

He was halfway through his popcorn when the lion tamer finished up, riding off stage on the back of the subdued animal. Russ expected the Ringmaster to reappear, but instead calliope music blasted through the loudspeakers as a group of six clowns rode out on unicycles as they juggled flaming batons. In the flickering light of the fires, their faces looked twisted and deformed, their eyes reflecting the flames as if the insides of their skulls were ablaze.

Russ found it suddenly hard to breathe, and the popcorn fell from his hands, landing at his feet and spilling all over the sticky floor. Despite the expansiveness of the near-empty Big Top, claustrophobia seized him by the throat and throttled him. This was silly; he was 37 years old, he shouldn't be afraid of clowns. And yet he was. He just kept thinking of the supernaturally animated stuffed clown that attacked the boy in *Poltergeist*.

He was actually thinking of getting up and leaving when the Ringmaster's voice came over the loudspeaker: "Ladies and gents, we have a special treat for you tonight. One lucky person has been chosen to come down and join our clowns, an audience participation sort of thing. And the lucky winner is..."

Russ prayed he wouldn't hear his name, but in his heart he knew he would. And he did.

No way I'm going down there, he thought, but his feet seemed to have a will of their own and carried him down the stands and out into the center ring. The clowns surrounded him, their demented faces full of malicious glee. Russ found himself trembling and he thought he might wet his pants.

Five of the clowns suddenly surged forward and took hold of him, their grip tight. He was sure they would leave bruises. He struggled against them but could not break away. Before him, the sixth clown laughed, the sound like breaking glass. The clown reached up and started to peel away its face, revealing that it had only been a rubber mask. Underneath was a face Russ recognized.

Charlie, from work.

"What's going on?" Russ asked in a tremulous voice.

Ignoring him, Charlie instead spoke to the other clowns. "Get him in position."

Before Russ could ask what that meant, the clowns turned him to see a scuffed wooden table that had appeared in the ring. Roughly, they shoved him over to the table and forced him to bend over it, splinters digging into his left cheek. As they held him down, Charlie came around to stand in his view. Russ gasped to see that Charlie's cock was exposed, standing at full attention and leaking a pearly liquid from the tip.

"Don't worry," Charlie said in a soothing tone. "I'm not going to put it in your mouth."

Then Charlie walked behind him as the clowns yanked Russ's pants and underwear down to his knees.

Russ started to scream, yelling out for those in the stands to help him. Instead, the audience started laughing, a few of them even hooting and applauding. His screams only intensified as he felt Charlie pushing in.

This can't be happening, he thought, but the pain told him it was. He thrashed on the table, trying to get loose of the clowns, but they held him tight. His scream became high-pitched and desperate. Behind him, he heard Charlie panting and saying, "Good boy, just take it. Relax, you'll learn to like it."

The stands were no longer nearly deserted. Russ was being violated to a packed house, and they were cheering so loud that they drowned out his own screams and pleas. He found himself praying for unconsciousness...

...and that was when he woke up. He was lying in his own bed, next to his wife. His pajamas were drenched in sweat, and his heart was trip-hammering in his chest as if it wanted to break loose. Becca was propped on her elbows, staring at him with concern in her eyes.

"Russ, what's wrong?"

"Oh Jesus, I just had the worst nightmare."

"What about?"

"I was at the circus, and there were all these clowns, and Charlie was there."

"Charlie? That nice gay guy from your office?"

"Yeah, and he—"

"He what?"

Russ hesitated. "Um, nothing, I can't really remember. It's already starting to fade."

"You sure you're okay?"

"Yeah," Russ said with a forced laugh. "It was just a dream. I'm going to go shower."

Standing under the hot spray, Russ tried to wash away the memory of the nightmare. Why would his imagination have conjured such a depraved scenario? Perhaps because he got the impression that Charlie had a crush on him. Nothing overt, just something in the way he looked at Russ, the way he talked to him. Vaguely flirtatious. Although Russ considered himself open-minded and accepting of all orientations, he had to admit being around Charlie made him uncomfortable. That must be where the dream stemmed from.

After he shaved and dressed, he walked into the kitchen. Becca had made pancakes for breakfast and they were waiting on the table. She was sitting there with a stack of bills and her checkbook. He felt a tightness in his gut, and the nightmare was forgotten in the light of his real world troubles.

"How bad is it?" he asked, taking a seat.

"Actually, the restaurant was really busy this weekend, and I made a killing in tips. I'm going to be able to pay the mortgage and at least cover the overdue amount on the power and water."

"Really? Well, that's a huge relief. And when I get my check this Friday I'll be able to pay the car and house insurance and get some groceries. That will at least take care of all that."

"That just leaves the phone bill and all these credit cards. We got a few more of those 'Pay now or we're turning your account over to our legal department' notices. But I'm hoping I have another good week in tips. I'll tell you, being all big and pregnant sure helps people loosen up their wallets."

Russ took a bite of his pancakes but found he didn't have much of an appetite. Pushing his plate away, he reached across the table and took his wife's hand. "Becca, I really don't think you should still be working. You shouldn't be on your feet so much."

"Russ, we've already been through this. We decided I'd work up to my eighth month."

"Yes, but—"

"No buts, you hear me? You know as well as I do that we're barely scraping by as it is. Once I go out on maternity leave it's only going to get worse. I've got to try to make all the money I can while I'm still able."

Russ wanted to argue, but he couldn't. She was right. They were horribly in debt, they'd already gotten rid of the cable and the Internet and all other luxury items. And still they had trouble paying the bills, and he was haunted by the fear that they might end up losing the house. It made him feel like a failure. Some old-fashioned part of him still considered it his responsibility as the husband to provide for the family, and he wasn't doing a very good job of it. And when the baby came, that was going to bring a whole new set of expenses.

Becca reached up and stroked her husband's cheek. "Hey, we're going to be okay. We'll do what we have to, but we're going to be okay."

With a smile, Russ said, "You know, when you say it, I almost believe it."

***

At a quarter 'til noon, Charlie stuck his head over Russ's cubicle wall and said, "I'm about to head out to lunch. Want me to grab you anything while I'm out?"

Russ looked up at Charlie but then quickly turned his eyes back to his computer screen. Images from last night's dream kept playing in his mind, no matter how hard he tried to wipe them away. He kept hearing Charlie saying, "*Good boy, just take it.*"

"No thanks, I'm fine. I brought some leftover meatloaf."

"You sure? My treat."

This last made Russ bristle. Did everyone view him as a fucking charity case? "Charlie, I said I'm fine. Okay?"

"Hey, no need to bite my head off. I was just being nice."

Russ took a moment and reeled his temper in. "I'm sorry, I just have a lot of work to do."

"Well, I'll leave you to it then."

As Charlie headed out of the office, Russ's memory conjured up another snippet from the dream: "*Relax, you'll learn to like it.*"

***

Charlie took a seat at his usual table in the very back corner of the restaurant. Becca came waddling over, her huge and perfectly round stomach leading the way. "Hi dollface," Charlie said with a smile.

Becca didn't return the smile. She pulled her pad and pen out of her apron. "What'll it be, Charlie?"

"I think a turkey club and a diet Pepsi. So, do you have something for me?"

Becca looked back toward the kitchen, making sure no one was watching. "Do you have the money?"

Charlie slid an envelope across the table. Becca snatched it up, opened it, and started counting the bills.

"It's all there," Charlie assured. "Two hundred dollars, just like the last time."

Reluctantly, Becca reached back into her apron and pulled out a sandwich baggie filled with tiny curly hairs that she'd fished out of the shower drain that morning. They were still damp. She felt nauseated at her own actions, but as she told her husband that morning, they would do what they had to do.

Charlie took the baggie and stuffed it in his pockets. "Thanks, and make sure to put the stone under his pillow again tonight."

Becca nodded, then blurted, "Russ dreamt about you last night."

Charlie merely stared at her for a moment. "And this is surprising?"

"Well, to tell the truth, I didn't really believe you could do it. I didn't really believe you could enter his dream like that."

"A relatively simple spell, as long as you have the right ingredients," Charlie said, patting his pocket. "Which you so graciously have been willing to provide."

Becca burned with shame, but she clutched the envelope full of money and it strengthened her resolve. They needed this money, and it wasn't as if anything were really happening to Russ. They were just dreams, after all.

"I'll go put in your order," Becca said, turning toward the kitchen. After two steps, however, she paused and looked back at Charlie. "You're not hurting him, are you?"

Charlie's smile was wide, and he winked at her. "Not at all. We're having a great time."

Dialogue is perhaps my favorite thing to write, and sometimes I really enjoy doing little pieces that are told entirely in dialogue. This one has a bit of a Lansdale flavor, a homage of sorts to a master storyteller.

Shootin' the Shit

"Zeke, I think ya killed 'er."

"Nah, she ain't dead, just playin' possum is all."

"Maybe ya hit 'er too hard."

"Sammy, ain't no such thing as hittin' a bitch too hard."

"Well, it just ain't as much fun when they dead."

"I told ya, she ain't dead. Look, her chest is movin' up and down."

"Yeah, I guess. Still, it's more fun when they awake."

"We ain't in no hurry, we can wait 'til she comes 'round."

"She's a pretty'un, that's for sure. You sure do pick 'em good, Zeke."

"A lot prettier than that hog you scored for us last time."

"I liked that'un. She was nice'n tight."

"Course she was. Nobody out there wanted to poke a pig like that."

"Well, she was sure nuff loose by the time we got done with 'er."

"So will this'un here, difference is I won't have to keep my eyes closed when I'm doin' it this time 'round."

"Ya sure she's still breathin'? She's bleedin' an awful lot from where ya bashed 'er with that baseball bat."

"What's it matter if she is or she ain't? Ya get your turn either way."

"Yeah, but it ain't as much fun when they dead."

"Still fun though, right?"

"I guess so."

"Tell ya what, Sammy, I'll let you go first."

"For real? You always go first."

"Not this time. No sloppy seconds for ya. She's all yours."

"Oh man, and a real knockout too. Can I do 'er now?"

"Thought ya wanted to wait 'til she was awake."

"I just can't wait, Zeke. Let me hit it now, please."

"Be my guest, lil' brother. Have at it."

"You won't watch, will ya? You know I have trouble when ya watch."

"Don't worry, I'll go over by them trees."

"'Kay. I'll holler when I'm done so you can come have your turn."

"Take your time. We got all night. Ain't like she's goin' nowhere."

This is an older piece I never had any luck selling, I think in part due to its subject matter. Which is, admittedly, disturbing, but I figure if you can't explore disturbing subject matter in horror, where can you explore it?

Urges

It wasn't planned. No matter what people might think later, Bradley hadn't left the house that morning intending to abduct the girl.

He'd never done anything like that before, never even contemplated it. Sure, there were those web sites he liked to visit on the 'net, and those pictures he kept stashed in the back of his closet, and those videotapes that had come wrapped in thick brown paper. But that was all make-believe, fantasies, not real.

But the little girl, she was real.

Her name was Katie, she was the nine-year-old daughter of Bradley's neighbors. Sometimes he found himself standing at the kitchen sink, staring out the small window, watching Katie jump rope in her backyard. He thought about that image at night, when his hands would stray beneath the covers.

But those, too, were just fantasies. They couldn't arrest a man for fantasies. He never planned to act on them.

But then he was driving home from work and there was Katie, walking down the street alone with a purple book-bag slung over her shoulder. It was blocks from their neighborhood, and no one seemed to be around.

Bradley pulled over to the curb, rolled down the passenger's window, and said, "Hey, Katie. It's me, Bradley, from next door."

"I know," she said, stepping close to the car. So trusting, so innocent, so ripe.

"What are you doing walking home?"

"I stayed after class to help Ms. Ericson clean the board, and I ended up missing the bus."

The saliva dried up in Bradley's mouth and the palms of his hands became damp as they gripped the steering wheel. "Want me to drive you home?" he finally asked.

"Sure," Katie said with a wide smile, opening the door and climbing into the car. Her plump little legs dangled over the seat, coming nowhere near reaching the floorboard. The right leg had a bandage on it, just below the knee.

"What happened there?" Bradley asked, reaching out and touching the bandage, wanting to slide his hand up the thigh but refraining.

"Got bit by a doggie when we went camping last month. Big, mean doggie. Had to get stitches and everything."

"How awful," Bradley said, pulling away from the curb. Even then, he wasn't planning to do anything but drop little Katie at her house.

But she ended up at Bradley's house, in the basement, a dirty rag he used to clean his shoes shoved in her mouth, her wrists and feet bound with electrical tape. Fantasies became reality in the darkness of the basement. The rag absorbed Katie's cries of protest and pain as Bradley gave in to the urges that had plagued him for years.

Later that night, Bradley sat out on his back porch, staring up at a blood-red moon that hung full and fat in the sky like a piece of rotting fruit. The police had come and gone next door. So far no one had come to ask him any questions. So he continued to sit, sipping a beer, staring at the night sky and contemplating.

He hadn't meant to take Katie; he hadn't meant to do those things to her. But he had, so now what? What was he going to do next?

He couldn't just let her go. She would tell. He couldn't have that. He didn't like to think of the alternative, but he had no choice. It was the only way.

Finishing off his beer, Bradley got up and went back inside. He pulled open one of the drawers in the kitchen and pulled out a large, shiny butcher knife. He tried not to think about what he was going to do, tried to put his mind on autopilot. After a few deep breaths, he headed for the basement.

As he descended the concrete stairs, he was stunned to see the card table was empty. He had left Katie tied and gagged on top of it, but now she was gone. As he stepped deeper into the room, he saw the rag and the shredded pieces of electrical tape littering the floor around the table. The tape had been wound tight, and she was so small and weak, how had she managed to get out of her bonds?

"Katie, doll, where are you?" he called out softly. At first there was no answer, but then he became aware of a low growling from behind him.

Bradley turned slowly, as if the air had thickened and was trying to hold him in place like amber, to discover a large black dog emerging from the shadows in the far corner. No, not a dog. A wolf.

Its fangs were bared, and it snarled and drooled as it inched forward. Bradley stared, slack-jawed, the knife forgotten in his hand.

Bradley just had time to register the bandage on the wolf's right hind leg before it pounced, snapping his neck between its massive jaws.

Another older piece, this one originally saw print in The Harrow *in 2005. This one I feel is a bit of homage to another master, Stephen King.*

Top of the World

Matt had never been on Top of the World.

Although the sixteen-year-old had been to the amusement park dozens of times, that was one attraction he always skipped. Top of the World was just a circular room with glass walls that ascended twenty stories in the air and spun slowly, offering a panoramic view of the park and surrounding area, before descending ever so leisurely back to ground level. Not much in the way of excitement. No loops or twists or water gushing at you. Matt considered it an old folk's ride.

It was the heat that drove Matt onto the ride this trip. Mid-July, and the temperature was in the hundreds, scorching the earth and draining energy as surely as vampires drained blood. The line for the park's one water ride was so long that it would mean an hour and a half wait in the blazing sun for fifteen minutes of riding down a manmade river with paper rocks and rubber trees. Didn't sound too promising.

And that left Top of the World. The circular room was air conditioned, and so many people could fit inside at one time that even if the line extended out the front gates of the park, the wait was still usually no more than half an hour. Seemed the surest way to beat the heat. Besides, there was always the chance that the attraction could malfunction and the circular room come crashing to the ground like an out of control UFO. That thought added a little excitement to the ride.

Matt took his place at the end of the line, mercifully standing in the shade of a nearby refreshment stand, and waited. The room was on its way down, and judging by the line ahead of him, Matt figured he just might make it into the room for the next trip. A young girl in front of him, surely no more than two years older than Matt himself, cradled a bawling baby in her arms. The child's high-pitched squeals drove into Matt's brain like icicles. The girl glanced over her shoulder and offered Matt an apologetic smile.

"It's the heat," she said. "Makes little Joe here cranky."

"I hear ya," Matt said. "We all get that way from time to time."

The girl pulled a pacifier out of her oversized purse and stuck it in the baby's mouth. Instantly the cries ceased as the child focused all its attention and energy onto sucking on the phony nipple.

Matt wiped sweat from his eyes and glanced up at the circular room. It was moving with excruciating slowness, which infuriated Matt right now but would no doubt offer him great solace when he was inside the room. He glanced at his watch as he waited. 4:15. His parents would be in the park's auditorium right about now, watching some country/western line dancing show. Matt would have suppressed his distaste for country/western and gone with them had the auditorium been indoors instead of the outdoor stadium it was.

With a resonating *clunk*, the room reached ground level and the automatic doors swooshed open. Those inside seemed reluctant to leave the comforting coolness of the circular room, finding some reason or other to linger inside, searching for lost items that did not exist, until the attendant asked them politely but firmly to exit the ride in a speedy manner. Matt could see the shock on the departing passengers' faces as the heat hit them like a solid wall.

After the room was emptied of its occupants, the attendant opened the small metal gate and allowed those in line to begin filing inside. Matt kept his fingers crossed, praying the room would not fill up before he got inside the doors. He didn't relish having to wait for the room to make another of its time-lapse-photography speed trips to the top of the world and back. As Matt drew closer to the doors, he cursed silently. The room had almost reached its capacity, and he wasn't sure he'd make this trip.

The girl ahead of him stepped through the doors and took a seat, her temporarily pacified baby sitting on her lap. There was a lone seat left, right next to the door. "Yes," Matt said loudly and lunged inside, taking the seat and smiling out at all those still waiting in line. He could certainly be a little snot when he wanted to be.

The automatic doors swooshed closed, and the blessed coolness wrapped itself around Matt like a tender embrace from a good friend he hadn't seen in a while. He turned to the girl beside him, euphoric smile on his lips, and said, "My name's Matt, Matt Henderson."

"Gloria Swenson," the girl said, bouncing the boy on her knees. "I believe you've already met Joe. It's his first trip to an amusement park."

"And are you having a good time, Joe?" Matt asked, playfully flicking a finger under the boy's chin, eliciting a trilling giggle from the child.

"Well, I'm not sure how good an idea it was to bring him," Gloria said. "I mean, there are only so many rides he can go on. We've been on the merry-go-round about a dozen times already. This is our third trip on Top of the World."

"I'm sure Joe is having the time of his life. Of course, there's not much competition at this point."

Gloria laughed. "Actually, I think today is more for me than him. I haven't gotten out much since Joe was born. Sometimes you just have to have a little fun."

There was a lurch and a low hum that increased in pitch, and the circular room began to rise. As it ascended into the heavens, the room also began to spin counter clockwise. Joe gasped delightedly, the pacifier dropping to his mother's feet. Gloria retrieved the nipple, blew on it absently, then popped it back into the child's mouth.

Matt leaned back in the cushiony seat, closing his eyes. He wasn't interested in the view; all that concerned him was this respite from the heat. His mind drifted, and he imagined he was standing underneath a waterfall of cool air, soothing and lulling him, cradling him as surely as Gloria cradled Joe in her maternal arms. Matt was not even aware that he'd dozed off until he was jerked awake by Gloria exclaiming, "Look, Joe, there's our car."

Matt wiped a line of drool from his chin and glanced out the glass. The room had reached its zenith twenty stories above the park and was revolving slowly. Matt looked down, experiencing a moment of unexpected vertigo. None of the other rides at the park went this high; in fact, Matt could see the other rides far below him, seeming at this distance like a child's toys discarded about the backyard. It was a cliché, but from this great height people did indeed look like ants, scurrying about the pencil-thin paths of the park. Matchbox cars lined the parking lot on the west end, and more rolled down the gray ribbon of highway in the distance. As the room continued to spin, Matt could see the open auditorium, filled with squirming ants. His parents were a couple of those ants.

"The world looks so neat from up here," Gloria said. "So organized. Not like real life at all."

Matt nodded and leaned back in his seat, studying the room's nondescript white metal ceiling. He was surprised by how unnerved Top of the World made him. He loved all the daredevil rides, the faster the better, but this ride, which he had always considered so benign, filled him with a childish fright. He was so high, suspended in the air, and the ride was moving so slowly. How easily something could go wrong. On most other rides, the experience was quick, too quick for one to devote much time to all the possible dangers. On Top of the World, Matt had ample time to consider every scenario that could lead to his eventual demise. He found himself praying the room would begin its decent soon.

Risking a quick glance out the glass, Matt saw the miniature world below spinning past at a faster rate. Roller coaster, auditorium, water ride, parking lot, roller coaster, auditorium, water ride, parking lot, roller coaster, auditorium, water ride, parking lot...

"I don't think it ever went quite this fast before," Gloria said with a laugh, but there was a certain edginess in her voice.

Matt found himself clenching his hands into tight fists as he watched the world rotate beneath him. He couldn't be sure, but he thought the circular room was continuing to pick up speed as it spun around. The rides and people on the ground were beginning to blur as they passed.

Joe began to cry again, scrambling into his mother's arms and burying his head in her chest. Gloria looked around, eyes wide, her breathing coming in harsh gasps.

"Is it supposed to do this?" Matt asked, surprised by the squeakiness of his voice.

"I don't think so," Gloria said, clutching her child to her, patting his back in a futile effort at comfort. "What's happening?"

The room was now spinning so fast that no features could be made out through the glass. It was all one great blur of kaleidoscopic color. Matt felt himself being pushed back against the seat by the force generated by the spinning room. It felt as if his skin was being peeled back from his face, and a frightfully detailed image came into his mind of his skin ripping completely off, leaving behind a bloody, grinning skull.

Matt heard gasps and screams from throughout the room, and what he thought was the Lord's prayer being recited nearby. He tried to turn his head, but he was stuck in place as if super-glued to the spot. It felt as if his insides were being forced out his back. Joe's cries became drowned out by the cries of the other passengers on the ride, and Matt realized his own screams were a part of the mix. He wanted to close his eyes but his lids would not shut. He found himself praying for the first time since he was seven years old. Nothing formal or eloquent, simply reciting a litany of promises to God, bargaining for his life: no more talking back to his mom, no more dirty magazines hidden under the mattress, no more taunting the mutt chained up next door, no more cheating on his math exams—

Matt was not initially aware of the room slowing, but then he realized he was staring at Gloria. He could still feel the force pushing against him, but he found he was able to lift his hands with some effort. The blur outside began to fall back into the normal patterns of the world. There was the sky, the sun making its trek toward the distant horizon; there was the ground far below, swaths of green with lines and blocks of gray cutting through them; there were the toy rides, colorful and bright.

"It's stopping!" he shouted, not sure if anyone could hear him. "The ride is stopping!"

Gradually the cries and prayers tapered as the rest of the passengers saw that the ride was indeed slowing. A loud hum and the circular room began its decent back to the world below. Cheers and applause greeted the reestablishment of normal proceedings.

Matt did not join in with the celebration. His eyes were focused on the park beneath them. The ride had seemed to come back on line, but something was still terribly wrong here.

Joe was still crying, but Gloria hugged him close, her own ecstatic tears spilling from her eyes. "Oh God, I was so scared," she was saying, speaking to no one in particular. "I thought that was it, I was dead. Me and poor Joe. I feel like I've been given a second chance. I'm going to make some changes in my life, that's for sure. No more taking things for granted. Oh, Matt, we made it."

"Did we?" Matt said absently, an unease building in the pit of his stomach and spreading throughout his limbs, numbing them. This was a fear deeper and more insidious than what he'd felt as the room spun out of control.

"What's wrong?" Gloria asked, seeing the expression of puzzlement and dread on Matt's face.

"Where are the people?"

Gloria followed Matt's gaze and saw what he saw, the park. Deserted. No one walked the cement paths, no one waited in line at the refreshment stands. The rides were frozen. The Ferris Wheel did not turn; the rollercoasters did not run; no water flowed in the log ride. The parking lot was still filled with cars, but nothing moved on the distant highway. The ants that Matt had seen scurrying around the park earlier were nowhere to be seen. The world seemed empty, no sign of any living creature.

Matt glanced around to see if anyone else had noticed the peculiar emptiness of the park, but everyone else seemed too overcome with relief to have studied the world outside the glass.

"Quite an adventure, huh?" said the attendant over the intercom, her voice tinny and hollow. "If you'll all remain in your seats until the ride comes to a full and complete stop, we should all be back on blessed solid ground in a few minutes."

As the room continued its decent, Matt leaned forward, hands splayed on the glass, leaving sweaty fingerprints behind, and squinted out at the world. Surely there must be someone down there; they couldn't have all vanished in a matter of moments. All the cars were still in the lot; where could everyone have gone? But his eyes remained insistent on what they saw, and what they *didn't* see. The park was deserted, a movie set before the actors had been called to the stage. Or after they'd gone home.

"Where is everyone?" Gloria asked, her voice a raspy hush. Even Joe had quieted, starting out the glass with wide-eyed wonder, as if even he had detected something amiss.

Other people started to notice. Whispers filled the circular room, and a mute panic spread throughout the confined space like a poisonous gas. Matt heard the intercom click on but the attendant said nothing, and after a moment of silence the intercom cut out again. The room had almost reached ground level, and Matt found himself wishing the room had remained twenty stories in the air. At least up there it had been easier to dismiss the park's emptiness as an optical illusion, a trick of his eyes and the distance.

But as the room reached the ground with a lurch and a *clunk*, there was no denying or rationalizing. The doors swooshed open on a vacant world.

At first no one moved. Everyone remained in their seats, silent and staring, statues with living eyes. Matt, closest to the door, was the first to move. Not out of any sense of leadership but simply because he couldn't stand to be in this little room anymore. Claustrophobia seized him around the throat and throttled him. He stood on wobbly legs and walked out the door. The air had cooled somewhat, a gentle breeze stirring the heat and soothing it. Matt walked through the metal gate and onto the main thoroughfare of the park. An empty potato chip bag scurried by Matt's feet, carried by the wind, making a faint hissing sound as it scraped along the pavement. It was this more than anything else that brought the reality of the situation to him, a tumbleweed rolling through the ghost town.

"Is it okay?"

Matt turned and saw Gloria, Joe in her arms, standing just inside the doorway of the ride. Others gathered behind her, as if afraid to take the step over the threshold.

"Is it okay?" Gloria asked again.

Matt didn't know how to answer that. The air wasn't poisonous; there were no man-eating beasts lying in wait; the ground hadn't opened beneath his feet and swallowed him up. But no, it wasn't okay. It wasn't anywhere near the vicinity of okay.

Gloria, taking a deep breath and closing her eyes, stepped out onto the pavement. She joined Matt outside the gate. Joe gurgled and squirmed, playfully tugging on his mother's hair.

"Hello?" Matt called out, expecting to hear his voice echoing back at him. Instead, the wind snatched the word away and carried it into the distance. Nothing greeted Matt but silence, an absence of sound so complete that Matt could almost believe they were in a soundproofed room and not outdoors. No sound of birds twittering in the trees; no dogs barking in the distance; no peripheral hum of airplanes passing overhead.

"What's happening?" Gloria said, startling Matt. He'd barely been aware of her next to him. "This can't be real, can it? I mean, where did they all go?"

"I don't know, but no one's here. That's all I do know for sure."

More people were making their way tentatively out of Top of the World. They milled about, slack-jawed and wide-eyed. A few clustered together and whispered. Everyone seemed afraid to speak loudly.

"Maybe we're dead," a balding man in Bermuda shorts and Top of the World T-shirt said, instantly gaining everyone's attention. "Maybe the ride broke and crashed, and we're all dead."

"And this is the afterlife?" asked a teenaged girl. "This is Heaven?"

"Or Hell," Bermuda Shorts said.

"This ride is fine," the attendant spoke up, standing just inside the gate, refusing to abandon her post as if walking over that threshold would cement the reality of this impossible situation. "It was thoroughly checked by our mechanics this morning, as it always is. There was nothing wrong with it; it was in perfect working condition."

"Oh yeah," Bermuda Shorts said, advancing on the attendant. "Then why the hell did it sling us around up there like a bunch of beans in a morocco? If it was so damn safe, why'd that happen? Huh?"

"Hey, hey, calm down," Matt said, taking Bermuda Shorts by the arm. The man spun around, eyes wild and frighteningly empty for a second. He seemed about to slug Matt in the face, but then his eyes focused and he regained his composure.

"Sorry," Bermuda Shorts said. "Just got a little carried away."

"It's understandable," Matt said. "But let's not lose our heads here. We need to stay calm and try to figure this out."

A woman in her fifties, silver hair neatly pinned at the nape of her neck, picked up a discarded Raggedy Ann doll from a wooden bench just off the path and said, "Maybe it was some kind of accident, a nuclear incident or something. I saw this *Twilight Zone* episode once where this guy was in a bank vault when a nuclear bomb wiped out the population and he was the only survivor. He walked out of the bank vault to find everyone gone and himself alone in the world."

"Doesn't hold water," said a man dressed in khaki shorts and a preppy polo shirt, mid-twenties/early-thirties to look at him. "A nuclear explosion would have wiped out all the buildings and cars in the area, but everything is still intact. And that ride, safe and sturdy as it may be," he added with a nod to the attendant, "is no bank vault. A nuclear incident would have disintegrated us as surely as everyone else."

"Maybe gas warfare," Silver Bun said. "We keep hearing about it, about the likelihood. Maybe they — Iraq or someone — released a poisonous gas into the atmosphere that killed everyone and then quickly dissipated. We were saved because we were on that ride, and by the time we made it back to the ground and the doors opened, the gas had lost its potency."

"Come on guys," screeched an overweight woman in a floral-patterned dress. "Let's face facts here. Everyone else was *abducted*."

"Oh goodness," Preppy Shirt said with a weary sigh. "Are you talking aliens?"

"What else?" Floral Dress waddled over to the bench and plopped down. "While we were stuck up on that hell ride, they came and took everyone else. Or maybe — "At this, she got so excited she almost teetered right off the bench. " — maybe *we* were the ones abducted. We've been placed on a replica of Earth where we are the only ones alive."

"Why would they do that?" Bermuda Shorts asked, a mixture of belief and disbelief showing on his face.

"To study us," Floral Dress said without missing a beat. "To study what we would do in such an extreme and otherworldly situation. Or maybe the government, maybe it is *our own government* who is conducting the experiment."

"Okay, okay, enough," Matt said, her rapid change of subject giving him mental whiplash. "This is getting us nowhere, let's try to keep our wits about us."

"Little whipper-snapper," Floral Dress mumbled, and Bermuda Shorts sat next to her and patted one of her truck-like arms.

A young man—no more than five years Matt's senior—with a military buzz-cut climbed up onto the stone wall that ran along the paved path, scanning the desolate park. "I suggest we split up and search the place," he said after a moment.

"What, you think everyone else is just playing a game of hide-and-go-seek?" Preppy Shirt said with a sneer. "We should all count to ten then go—"

Buzz Cut shot a heated glance that shut Preppy Shirt up instantly. "Listen up, everyone. We could sit around all day trading speculations and quips, but that doesn't seem very productive to me. This place *looks* to be abandoned, yes, and maybe it is, but what I'm suggesting is that we don't just take that for granted. I say we make sure, see if there is *anyone* else in the park. Now I can't force you to go along with me on this, but anyone who wants to raise your hand."

At first no hands went up. Then the attendant's hand rose slowly in the air. Then Silver Bun's hand. Then another, and a few more. Matt's hand was one of the ones raised. Gloria stood next to him, holding Joe in one arm and raising the other above her head. In all, a little more than half of the people had raised their hands.

"Good," Buzz Cut said. "The rest of you can sit around here, pick lint out of each other's bellybuttons, whatever the hell you want to do. The rest of us are gonna check things out. You two," he said, pointing to a gay couple in matching Hawaiian shirts, "you'll come with me. We'll check out the parking lot. You three over there, why don't you go to the Pavilion and check out the stores. And you two..."

Buzz Cut went down the line, assigning areas for everyone with the total confidence of someone used to being in charge, used to giving orders and having them followed. Matt didn't mind. It felt good to have someone be in charge, gave the impression of order in all this chaos. Buzz Cut suggested (*ordered*) Matt and Gloria to see what they could find at the auditorium.

"It's a mistake to split up," Preppy Shirt started yelling. "You guys probably won't come back. We should just all stay here."

"And do what?" Buzz Cut said, staring Preppy Shirt down. Without another word, he motioned for the gay couple and the three of them headed toward the parking lot.

"You'll see," Preppy Shirt called out after Buzz Cut was a good distance away. "You'll all disappear, and then you'll be sorry."

Floral Dress started to cry on the bench, Bermuda Shorts wrapping his arms as far around her as he could get them.

"Well, guess Joe's first trip to the park is memorable," Matt said as he and Gloria separated from the group and headed downhill toward the auditorium.

"Guess so," Gloria said with a weak, unconvincing laugh. "I still can't believe any of this is real. I keep thinking I must have fallen asleep on Top of the World, and any minute the attendant is going to shake me awake and ask me to exit the ride."

Matt reached out and gave Gloria's hand a gentle squeeze. "I know what you mean. It's like we've stepped into some Stephen King novel or something."

Gloria shivered and held Joe closer to her bosom. "His books always end badly."

Matt could think of no response to that, so the two of them walked the rest of the way in silence.

The auditorium was a round structure, made to look like an ancient Roman coliseum. For the first time, it struck Matt how perverse this was, as if people were lining up not to see some country singer or kiddie show but Christians devoured by lions.

Of course, there were no lines today. Matt and Gloria pushed through the turnstile and into the lobby area. There was a ticket booth, a table with stacks of programs, a gift shop—all empty. Their footsteps were loud in the stillness of the place.

"What do you think is happening?" Gloria asked in a whisper, a church voice. "I mean, *really*?"

Matt paused before answering, considering. Finally, he just shrugged and said, "I honestly have no clue. I wish I did, but I just have no clue."

Joe had fallen asleep in his mother's arms, and Gloria bounced him gently up and down as they stepped through one of the large archways into the auditorium itself. Bleachers descended downward, encircling a center stage. Overhead the sky was a dull blue. Programs and paper cups littered the bleachers and aisles, but there were no people to read the programs or drink the beverages. It was as if everyone had just gotten up in the middle of the show and hightailed it out of there, including the performers.

Matt sank down onto one of the bleachers, his breath coming in ragged hiccups, a few tears streaming down his cheeks. He had managed to hold it together thus far, but seeing the deserted auditorium finally broke through his manufactured calm.

"Matt, are you okay?" Gloria asked, placing a hand on his shoulder. "What's wrong?"

"My parents were here," Matt said, taking a napkin he found lying next to a half-eaten bag of popcorn and discreetly blowing his nose. "They came to see the line dancing show, so they would have been here when...well, when whatever happened happened."

"I'm sorry," Gloria said, leaving her hand on Matt's shoulder. She opened her mouth as if to say more, but then she just shook her head, looked away, and said again, "I'm sorry."

"Well, no use crying about it," Matt said, wiping his eyes with the napkin and rising to his feet. "Tears won't change anything. I guess we head back to Top of the World and report that the auditorium is as empty as everything else."

"Yeah, but maybe someone else will have found something."

"Stranger things have happened," Matt said with a smile and the two left the auditorium.

The silence on the return trip was more companionable, more comfortable than before. They stopped at a refreshment stand, went behind the counter, and fixed themselves some drinks. Joe sucked greedily at a bottle Gloria pulled from her shoulder bag. By the time they got back to the ride, most of the others had already returned.

"Nothing," Matt told Buzz Cut. "There was stuff around, drink and snacks, as if people had just been there, but there was no one."

"That seems to be the consensus all around," Buzz Cut said with a frown. "I'm afraid appearances were *not* deceiving in this instance. This amusement park seems to be as deserted as it first appeared. And there's nothing moving on the highway, which leads me to believe we'd find more of the same elsewhere."

"Impossible," Silver Bun said, clutching a jade necklace that hung around her neck. "What are you suggesting, that the *whole world* is empty?"

"I'm not suggesting anything, just telling you what I know. And what I know is that there is no traffic on the highway, not a single vehicle."

"Well, we need to get out of here," Silver Bun said, eliciting murmurs of agreement from the crowd. "Let's just get in our cars and see if we can find help."

"You're free to give it a try," Buzz Cut said to the crowd. "But I tried my car, and these two fellows tried theirs, and it was a no-go."

"What do you mean?" Bermuda Shorts asked. "A no-go?"

"Our cars wouldn't crank."

"More than that," one of the Hawaiian Shirts added. "I mean, the engine didn't even make a sound. There was no whirring or coughing, it was as if there was nothing under the hood."

"Did you look under the hood?" Bermuda Shorts said. "No offense, but your kind aren't the most adept when it comes to automobiles."

"I took a look under their hood and my own," Buzz Cut said. "As far as I could tell, everything was in working order, nothing tampered with, nothing broken. Only the cars *wouldn't* work, they simply wouldn't start. Like I said, if any of the rest of you want to give it a shot, feel free. Maybe you'll have better luck than us, although something tells me not."

"We reached a decision while you were gone," Preppy Shirt said, stepping toward Buzz Cut. The stances of the two men reminded Matt of some shoot-out in an old Western movie.

"And that would be what?" Buzz Cut asked.

"We're gonna go back up, back up in Top of the World."

"What?" Gloria asked, patting Joe gently but firmly on the back. "Why would you do that?"

"All of this started because of that damn ride." When the attendant opened her mouth to protest, Preppy Shirt quickly added, "For whatever reason, going up in Top of the World seemed to have caused this situation."

"But me and Joe have ridden that ride a lot today. Nothing like this happened before."

"Well, what do you think caused it?" Preppy Shirt said, his voice rising and his nostrils flaring. "Huh, little girl?"

"I suggest you mind your manners," Matt said, stepping between Preppy Shirt and Gloria. "She was just making an observation; there's no need for you to get so bent out of shape. And there is no excuse for talking to a lady like that."

"Well, aren't you the chivalrous little piss-ant," Preppy Shirt said with a laugh, advancing on Matt. "I'll talk to anyone anyway I please, you got that."

Buzz Cut grabbed Preppy Shirt by the arm and spun him around to face him. "Why don't you pick on someone your own size instead of a couple of kids?"

Matt thought about protesting that he wasn't a kid, but then thought it was a good idea to just let Buzz Cut handle the situation.

"I wasn't gonna do nothing to them," Preppy Shirt said, yanking his arm loose from Buzz Cut's grip. "But we all know that *somehow* being on Top of the World got us in this predicament. Maybe going back on the ride will fix it."

"Or it could make things much worse," Buzz Cut said. "I don't recommend it."

"You don't *recommend* it?" Preppy said with an incredulous laugh. "I know that for some reason you seem to think you're the boss, but I don't give a shit what you recommend. I say our best bet is to go back on the ride."

"Maybe he's right," the attendant said timidly. "I don't know how the ride could be responsible for any of this, but if it is then maybe the only way to get out of it is to go up again."

"I agree," Floral Dress said, Bermuda Shorts nodding beside her like a bobble-head doll. "We need to go back on the ride."

"Of course you're all free to do what you want," Buzz Cut said, sitting down on the stone wall. "I'm staying put. I just think it's too risky. This time it could spin right off and crash back down to the ground."

"Or maybe you just don't want to be proven wrong," Preppy Shirt said. "Show of hands, who all wants to go back up on the ride?"

Matt looked around. Everyone had raised their hands expect for himself, Buzz Cut, and Gloria.

"You think maybe we should go back up?" Gloria said, stepping up close to Matt. She had latched on to him for some reason, and it was obvious she would do whatever he did.

"I don't know, I just think he's right about it being risky. After how the ride lost control the last time, it just seems unnecessarily dangerous to go back on it."

Gloria looked down at Joe, who grabbed her nose and laughed. "I guess you're right."

"Fine," Preppy Shirt was saying. "I hope you three are very happy here, all alone in your empty world. The rest of us are getting the hell out of here."

The crowd started filing back into the circular room. Matt sat on the stone wall next to Buzz Cut. The two exchanged a glance but did not speak. Gloria stood nearby, rocking Joe and watching the room fill up. Just before the doors swooshed closed, she turned to Matt and said, "I'm sorry, I've got to go with them. Come with me."

"I just don't think it's safe," Matt said. "I think we're better off down here."

"I've got to go," she repeated, backing down the path toward the ride. "I can't just wait around here, I'm sorry."

Joe began to cry, loud and high-pitched, as Gloria turned and rushed down the path, yelling, "Hold the door, I'm coming." She got through the door just before it closed. The sun beat off the glass, making it impossible to see inside.

The hum started, the room beginning its slow spinning ascent into the heavens. Matt watched it rise, remembering how desperate he'd been to get inside earlier, back when the world had made sense.

"You could have gone with your girlfriend if you wanted," Buzz Cut said. "I mean, there's nothing that says I'm right about this."

"She's not my girlfriend," Matt said absently, not taking his eyes off the ride as it rose high above them. It was now at the midway point.

Buzz Cut walked over to the nearby refreshment stand and came back with two large soft pretzels. Without a word, he handed one to Matt, who took it also without a word. The two sat there, munching on the salty treats, watching Top of the World reach the top of the world and spin slowly.

The room stayed there at the zenith, spinning slowly at its normal speed, for about three minutes before it began its decent. There had been no out of control spinning this time.

"Looks like nothing happened," Matt said, finishing his pretzel and tossing the wrapper in a nearby wastebasket.

"I'm sure that jackass will be so disappointed," Buzz Cut said bitterly. This was a man who obviously did not like having his authority questioned, and it occurred to Matt that perhaps it had been foolhardy to blindly follow this man's lead.

The circular room finally reached ground level and came to a halt. The door opened, and Matt waited for Gloria to emerge with Joe in tow. A minute passed, two, three, and no one exited the ride.

Matt and Buzz Cut looked at one another then stood and walked toward the ride. There was no one inside; the room was empty. They walked around the entire room, but everyone was gone. Vanished. Just by the door, Matt bent and reached under the seat, pulling out Joe's pacifier. He stared at it for a moment, then walked out into the empty park.

"Damn fools," Buzz Cut said, following behind. "I tried to warn them. Now they've disappeared too, just like everyone else."

"Maybe they're back *with* everyone else," Matt said, clutching the pacifier in his fist as if it gave him a connection to Gloria and her child. "Maybe when the room descended for them, the doors opened onto a park full of people."

"Or maybe they're in some awful limbo," Buzz Cut said. "Or maybe they're spinning around in that room for eternity. Point is, we have no way of knowing. There is no telling what happened to them, where they went. We made the right call staying behind."

Matt said nothing, just stood there with the pacifier in his hand, staring back at the empty room.

"Look, kid, I'm going to head off down the highway, see if the old woman was right. Maybe there are people out there. If so, I'm going to find them. You can tag along with me if you want."

Buzz Cut stood there for a few minutes, awaiting a response. When he didn't get one, he turned, mumbled "Suit yourself," over his shoulder, and headed off toward the parking lot and the highway beyond.

Matt stayed frozen in place, eyes flickering between the open door of Top of the World and the receding back of Buzz Cut. Matt chewed on his lower lip, trying to force his chaotic mind to come to a decision.

Finally, taking a deep breath, Matt started to move.

This was the result of a flash fiction challenge. I enjoyed telling this very irreverent and I think humorous creation tale. Makes more sense to me than the traditional one.

The Day that God Threw Up

God wasn't feeling all that well. He shifted on his throne, his stomach making a sick grumbling sound like thunder. He shifted again, broke wind, and thought he felt something damp in his shorts.

"Oh no," he moaned.

Michael paused in his work. He had been scooting the push-broom around the throne room; there had been a Hosanna sing-along with the angels earlier, and the place was lousy with shed feathers. "Something wrong, your Majesty?"

God felt sweat trickling down his face, and when he at first tried to speak all that came out was a juicy belch. "I think the Ambrosia I had for dinner was bad."

"I had the same thing, and I feel just fine."

"Well, something is wrong with me. Maybe Lucifer spiked my wine; I swear that imp has it out for me."

"Lord, all the angels adore you. Why, they practically worship you."

More rumbling from his stomach, and God grabbed his abdomen as he was seized with intense cramps. "I'm going to barf, I can feel it. Quick, Michael, bring me a bucket."

"Why not use the empty Earth habitat?"

Ah yes, Earth. God had originally created it as a game preserve for his little pets, reptilian creatures of various types which he had named dinosaurs. Unfortunately, last week he'd been flipping a coin when trying to decide what sandals to wear, but instead of catching it, the coin had hit his thumb then bounced into the habitat, and the heavy thing had raised such a dust storm in the enclosure that all the creatures had ended up dying. God still felt awfully guilty about that, and had just left the habitat empty, not having the heart to fill it with more pets.

Which was fortuitous, as it sat right next to the throne and he didn't even have to stand. He just leaned over, opened his mouth, and spewed forth a stream of foul-smelling bile into the habitat. Chunks of the Ambrosia he'd eaten earlier poured out of him, along with chunks of breakfast as well. He vomited so long, he was sure he was expelling everything he'd eaten in the past millennia.

But finally it passed, and he collapsed back in his chair, gasping, exhausted the way one feels after sickness. And yet he was definitely feeling better. Whatever had caused him to be so ill, he had purged himself of it.

"Michael, be a dear and take Earth and clean it out, would you?"

"Of course, your Majesty."

Michael reached out to pick up the habitat but then paused. "Lord, there's something…in there."

"Yes, my sick."

"No, I mean there's something in the sick, looks like little creatures squirming around in the bile."

Curious, God leaned forward again, grimacing at the sour smell emanating from Earth. Michael was right, there were little maggot-like creatures in his vomit, struggling to rise out of the slimy mess. That must have been what was making him sick.

"I'll get rid of this right away," Michael said.

God held up a hand. "Not so fast. I am intrigued."

"By parasites that made you ill?"

"Yes. Just look at them, there are so many of them. I wonder how intelligent they are, how they will get along, how they will progress. I think I'll keep them."

"Keep them, your Majesty?"

"Indeed. I need some new pets after all. I think I'll call them Man."

This was also the result of a writing challenge, and one of my non-horror pieces. I just wanted to explore the feeling of being trapped by circumstances, doomed to a certain kind of life. There's a bleakness to this piece, yet I really enjoyed writing this one. These kids felt real to me, and I found myself hoping for the best for them...

Welcome to the Graveyard

Being the new kid in school sucked. Almost as much as being the principal's son. Seth Hammond had both strikes against him, making those first two weeks at Paddington High a rough experience. The other kids treated him coolly at first, simply because he was new; he hadn't grown up with these people, didn't know their stories, and was therefore not to be trusted. After only a few days, Seth's father proved himself to be a stern and unpopular principal, and the other students' coolness toward Seth turned into outright animosity. Guilt by association.

Over breakfast the Friday morning of Seth and his father's second week at Paddington, Seth took a deep breath and said, "Dad, would you mind if I started walking to school?"

Mr. Hammond paused in the process of buttering his toast and looked at his son as if he were a particularly difficult geometry problem. "Why would you want to do that?"

"Well, it's only four blocks away."

"Yes, and I drive there every morning. Why walk when you can just ride with me?"

Seth realized too late that he hadn't thought this through enough, finding no response handy. Finally he just blurted, "The exercise will be good for me."

Mr. Hammond snorted a laugh. "That's the best you could come up with?"

Seth said nothing, but heat suffused his face and he just knew he had turned bright red.

Putting down his butter knife, Mr. Hammond wiped his hands on his napkin and said, "You wouldn't be ashamed of being seen with your father, would you?"

"It's not that, Dad. It's just..."

"Just what? You can tell me."

Seth ducked his head down, as if expecting a punch. "It's just no fun being the principal's kid."

"I realize that, but whether I drive you to school or not, you're still going to be the principal's kid."

"I know," Seth mumbled, shoveling a spoonful of Cheerios into his mouth and avoiding his father's gaze.

"Is there anything else bothering you, son?"

Seth planned to say nothing, but he felt everything he'd been holding down suddenly bubbling up toward the surface. He tried to hold it back, but there was no stopping this flood. "I hate it here! I don't have any friends, all the kids at school treat me like I'm some kind of spy, and this pathetic excuse for a town doesn't even have a mall or movie theater to go to. I wish we'd never come here!"

Risking a peek up at his father, Seth saw hurt and anger warring on the man's face. Anger won out. "You think you're the only one having a rough adjustment? You think I'm not having a hard time being in a new place at a new job? You think I didn't leave all my friends behind as well? I never wanted to move to a town as small as Paddington, and I certainly didn't want to transfer so far away from Seattle, but this was the only job opening I could find on such short notice."

"I don't see why you couldn't have just kept your job at Cornelius High back in Washington."

Mr. Hammond fixed his son with a withering glare, and Seth instantly wished he had kept his mouth shut. He understood why his father had sought a transfer. His wife, Seth's mother, was the Phys Ed teacher at Cornelius, and last spring she had left her husband and son and moved in with Bret Randolph, the new biology instructor that Mr. Hammond had personally hired. Seth himself would have found it hard to walk down the halls and see his mother and her new lover; he couldn't imagine how much more difficult it would be for his father.

And thus Paddington High in Paddington, South Carolina.

When Mr. Hammond continued to glare in silence, Seth carried his bowl to the sink and stammered a timid, "I'm sorry," as he passed his father.

"I need to go," Mr. Hammond said, leaving his own dishes on the table for his son to clear. "I have to be in early today. You can walk over when you've finished getting ready."

Mr. Hammond left the kitchen without a goodbye or even a glance in his son's direction. Seth stood alone by the sink, feeling like an ass.

***

He was running late. He spent too much time trying to pick out something to wear that wouldn't make him look like a complete dork while also not making him look like he put too much consideration into his outfit. By the time he settled on a faded pair of jeans and a T-shirt with the logo of a band he hoped was still cool on the front, he only had ten minutes to get to Paddington High before the first bell. Even with the school only four blocks away, that was pushing it.

Still, Seth didn't rush; he was in no hurry to get to school. So what if he was a little late for homeroom? Sure, he'd catch hell from his father, but that was nothing new. Mr. Hammond hadn't been like this back in Seattle, before Seth's mother had walked out on them. He'd been fun and somewhat lenient, and he had been much loved by the students at Cornelius High. But since the divorce and the subsequent move, Mr. Hammond had turned bitter and angry, a taskmaster at both school and home. Seth was sixteen years old, and his father chose now to start treating him like a child.

He shuffled his feet along the cracked sidewalk, his backpack hanging heavy on his shoulder, as if it were filled with rocks instead of books. Up ahead, he could see the two-story, rectangular brick building that was the town's high school. The elementary school Seth had attended back in Seattle was larger than Paddington High, and the school boasted only one hundred and fifty students, and that included all four grades. Seth's father had moved them not only to the middle of nowhere, but the middle of the middle of nowhere.

While still half a block from the school, he heard the shrill bell signaling the beginning of the school day. Now Seth did pick up the pace, half-jogging the rest of the way. As he turned up the cement walk that led to the school's front entrance, he skidded to a stop so abruptly he almost tripped over his own feet. Sitting on the front steps, dressed in leather jackets and smoking, were Dirk Yates and his cronies. A half dozen seniors—a few of them, including Dirk, nineteen years old due to having been held back—who seemed to model themselves after every bully in every teen movie that had ever been made. They were all bad attitudes, sneering lips, and threatening postures. Seth had heard a rumor that last year Dirk had beaten up a freshman so badly that he'd put the boy in the hospital. Seth didn't know if it were true or not, but he didn't discount it out of hand.

"Well, look who we got here, it's Hammond," Dirk said, taking a final drag on his cigarette and tossing it into the bushes. "The principal's own son, late for school. Not exactly setting a good example for the rest of us students, are you?"

Dirk's cronies laughed, the sound oily, and Seth just trained his eyes on the walk in front of him and headed for the door. The leather-clad seniors did not move from their perch on the steps, blocking his way.

"Or maybe the rules don't apply to you," Dirk said. "Is that it? Since you're Hard-ass Hammond's son, you automatically got a 'Get Outta Jail Free' card or something?"

Seth shook his head. "I'm just running behind, is all."

"That right? Bet they'll be hell to pay at home tonight, huh? As strict as Hard-ass is here at school, I bet he's ten times worse at home. Am I right? He strikes me as the type that probably keeps his kid locked up in a broom closet and beats him with a razor strap. If I yanked your pants down right here in front of God and everybody, would your ass cheeks be covered with welts?"

Seth felt himself trembling with a mixture of fury and fear. While he hadn't exactly been Mr. Popularity back at Cornelius, he'd had a tight-knit group of friends. Everything was different now, and at Paddington he found himself King Geek, though no one picked on him quite as much as Dirk's little gang of misfits and malcontents.

Dirk stood, towering over Seth by a good three inches. "How about it, Hammond? Does your daddy beat your tender little ass 'til it's sore, or does he do something else to make it sore?"

Seth wanted to back away but forced himself to stand his ground. "Just let me by," he said, his voice coming out with a quaver despite his best efforts. "We're all late for homeroom."

More slimy-slick laughter, and Dirk took a step closer. "You wanna get by, all you gotta do is pay the toll."

"What?"

"The toll. To get by us, it's gonna take...how much do you guys think we should charge?"

"A hundred bucks," said one of Dirk's buddies, a chubby kid with the round, doughy face of a Cabbage Patch doll.

Dirk smiled and shook his head, his eyes never leaving Seth. "Nah, Ryan, no need to be that greedy. We're reasonable men. Let's say twenty bucks. Twenty bucks and you can walk right by us."

Seth looked around the school grounds, hoping for someone to come along, but of course everyone else was safely tucked away in homeroom. If Seth had just ridden with his father like usual none of this would be happening. "You want me to pay you just to go in the building?"

"No, I want you to pay me for *letting you* go in the building."

"That's ridiculous."

One more step, and now Dirk was standing directly in front of Seth, staring down at him with an intensity rarely seen outside of mental wards. "What you gonna do, tell your daddy on us?"

"Nuh-no, of course not," Seth stammered, disgusted by the way he cringed back from Dirk. "I just need to get inside."

Dirk walked backwards and returned to his seat on the steps with his friends. "Well, you ain't getting through this door. Not unless you pay the toll."

Seth stood there for a moment, wishing he were stronger, braver, more of a man. He wanted to stand up to Dirk and prove that he wasn't some pussy who could be pushed around, but he was afraid of ending up like the possibly fictitious freshman from last year.

In the end, Seth turned without a word and started across the grass, heading for the side of the building. He was afraid Dirk and his cronies would follow him, but they remained on the front steps, their laughter ringing out like accusations of cowardice. Seth entered the school from the back entrance by the cafeteria and hurried to homeroom.

***

Seth walked down the deserted hallway, his footsteps sounding as loud as gunshots. The hall pass, a thick square of wood with the words HALL PASS engraved on each side, was clutched in his hand. He'd hoped to make it until lunch before having to use the restroom, but halfway through third period the pressure on his bladder had become urgent and undeniable. He hated raising his hand and calling attention to himself, but he'd asked for the hall pass and hurried out of the classroom, feeling eyes of judgment weighing on his back. It was stupid, really. Everybody had to use the bathroom; there was no reason he should feel so conspicuous and freakish, but it didn't change the fact that he did.

The nearest restroom was down the hall by the industrial arts workshop. He pushed open the swinging door and stepped inside, instantly enveloped in the stench of urine, bleach, and stale cigarette smoke. When he saw Dirk and Ryan—he of the Cabbage Patch face—leaning against the trough-like sink, Seth cursed his bad luck and almost backpedaled quickly out the door.

"Hey, it's Hammond again," Dirk said, taking a drag on his cigarette, smoke leaking from his nostrils in twin streams. "You following me around or what?"

"He must be in love with you," Ryan said with a moronic giggle. "He probably was hoping to get a peek at your pecker by following you into the john."

"That it, Hammond? You wanna get a look at my junk?"

Despite his humiliation, Seth still desperately needed to urinate. He dropped the hall pass on top of the garbage can and hurried to the urinals, lined up on the opposite wall across from the sink. Usually he found it hard to urinate when there were others in the bathroom, but the need to go was so great that he had no trouble today, even though he could practically *feel* Dirk and Ryan watching him. When he was done, he zipped up quickly and turned to grab the hall pass.

Which was now in Dirk's hands.

"Leaving so soon?" Dirk said, eliciting another giggle from his buddy. "Not even gonna offer to show me yours if I show you mine?"

"I need to get back to class." Seth made a grab for the hall pass, but Dirk jerked it away.

"Hey, Hammond, I'm not judging. In this day and age, everybody knows it's okay to be queer."

"Maybe you could even make us over like those fags on that TV show," Ryan said.

Seth considered just leaving and telling Mrs. Gambrell that he'd forgotten the hall pass in the restroom, but then she'd probably just send him back for it. "Come on, you guys, I really have to get back."

Dirk handed the hall pass to Ryan, took another drag on his cigarette, then set it on the edge of the sink. "Tell you what, if you can get by me, Ryan will give you the hall pass."

"What do you mean, if I can get by you?"

"Just what I said. You try to get to Ryan, and I'll try to block you. If you —"

Dirk was interrupted when the restroom door swung open and Mr. Hammond stepped inside. He looked at the three students and seemed to deduce what was going on in an instant. "Trouble?" he asked, directing the question toward his son.

Seth shook his head. "No, sir. I had to use the restroom. I was just about to head back to Chemistry."

"You'll need this," Mr. Hammond said, stepping toward Ryan to retrieve the hall pass. He paused when he saw the burning cigarette on the rim of the sink. "Well, what do we have here?"

Seth saw Dirk's eyes widen in what looked like fear, an emotion of which he hadn't thought the bully capable.

After extinguishing the butt under the tap and tossing it in the garbage, Mr. Hammond turned his attention to Dirk and Ryan. "Seth, you run on back to class now while I try to determine which of these two punks was smoking on school grounds. I foresee suspension in someone's future. Expulsion if it turns out to be Mr. Yates, as this would be his third offense."

Dirk pulled a mask of contempt over his fear and opened his mouth to say something, but before he could speak, Seth blurted, without giving it much thought, "It was me."

His father, Dirk, and Ryan all stared at Seth with identical expressions of slack-jawed disbelief. It would have been comical under other circumstances. Finally Mr. Hammond found his voice and said, "Seth, since when do you smoke?"

"I don't do it often, just every now and then. It's not like a habit or anything, I swear."

Mr. Hammond looked suspiciously at Dirk, who just raised his hands and said, "Hey man, I tried to tell him it wasn't cool to be breaking the rules."

"I'm sure you did."

"You know what they say, a bad apples makes all the rest of us look bad." Dirk couldn't keep a grin off his face; he was obviously enjoying this.

"You two get back to class," Mr. Hammond said, then took his son by the shoulder. "Seth, you come with me."

Before he could say anything else, Seth was shoved through the door and escorted to the principal's office.

***

Seth was in his father's office for almost an hour, enduring a lecture of apocalyptic proportions. To hear Mr. Hammond tell it, smoking led to everything from cancer to heroin to the end of civilization altogether. Seth suffered it all with a suitable look of contrite shame, all the while wanting to tell his father he'd never touched a cigarette in his life, but something holding him back. He wasn't exactly sure why he'd taken the blame, but it seemed a combination of several factors. Anger at his father for the way he'd been treating Seth as of late. Fear of what retribution Dirk might seek if he were kicked out of school. And, most surprising, actual sympathy for the bully.

His lunch period was nearly over when Seth finally left the office, feeling exhausted from the verbal lashing he'd taken. He'd just started down the hallway toward the cafeteria, hoping there was enough time to catch a quick bite before English Composition, when he heard someone behind him call his name. Turning, he saw Dirk walking his way; he'd apparently been waiting just outside the office.

"What do you want now?" Seth said, not at all in the mood to put up with more of the bully's shit at the moment.

Dirk cleared his throat, put his hands in his pockets, took them back out, popped his knuckles, put his hands in his pockets again. He seemed fidgety and unsure of himself, something Seth had never witnessed before. "I just wanted, you know, to say that it was awful decent of you to take the bullet for me like that."

Seth shrugged and said, "No problem," though he really wanted to say, *I was scared you'd kick my ass otherwise.*

"Yeah, my ma would've had a shit-fit if I got expelled this early in the school year."

"What, she prefer you to get expelled closer to graduation?"

Dirk laughed uncertainly. "Good one, Hammond."

Seth nodded, checked his watch, listened to his stomach grumbling. "Well, I guess I'll see you around."

"Wait a minute. I was just wondering, me and some of the guys are gonna be hanging out tonight at the Graveyard, I thought you might wanna join us."

Seth was instantly on guard, wondering if this was some set-up to humiliate him further. "Why would you want to hang out with me?"

Some of Dirk's bad-boy swagger returned, and he lifted one shoulder in a half-shrug that seemed to say, *I couldn't give a shit either way.* "Look Hammond, you did me decent, I'm just trying to return the favor."

"Well, thanks. I appreciate the offer, but I'm pretty much grounded from now until I start collecting Social Security."

"So what? I've spent most of my teen years grounded, ain't never stopped me from going out."

"I don't know. I think maybe—"

"Hold on a second," Dirk said, sudden laughter quaking through his body. "Are you telling me you ain't never snuck out before?"

Embarrassed, though he couldn't say why, Seth just shook his head.

Dirk came up and put his arm around Seth's shoulders, leading him on down the hall. "Dude, I got to you just in time. I got a lot to teach you."

***

Just after midnight, Seth eased up his bedroom window and climbed out. He couldn't believe he was doing this; it was like some scene in a movie. His father was asleep—he hoped—just across the hall. If he were to catch Seth sneaking out...well, Seth didn't even want to finish that thought.

So why was he doing it? Seth was a normal sixteen-year-old in that he had indulged in the usual assortment of disobedience and rebellion, but nothing serious. For the most part, he was a good kid, square as that sounded. But being good got rather old after a while, and despite the fear of getting caught, he had to admit that it was somewhat thrilling to be doing something he wasn't supposed to.

Besides, this was the first time since he and his father had moved to Paddington that Seth had been invited to join in anyone's reindeer games. Dirk wasn't exactly the type that he was accustomed to hanging out with, but at this point the prospect of a friend—*any* friend—was just too enticing to refuse.

Once outside, Seth closed the window most of the way, leaving just a crack so it would be easier to get the window back up when he returned. He paused to glance through the glass at his bed, wondering if he should have stuffed pillows under the covers, but that was silly. As far as he knew, his father never checked on him in the night, and if he did, he wasn't likely to be fooled by something so *Ferris Bueller's Day Off*.

Pulling the crinkled slip of paper out of his pocket, Seth checked the address Dirk had given him earlier in the day. The corner of Glenavon and Studemont. Seth didn't think it was but a few blocks away, although in a town the size of Paddington, *everything*

192 | Mark Allan Gunnells

was only a few blocks away. Moving with exaggerated stealth, he made his way around the side of the house, going the long way to avoid his father's bedroom window. Once he was at the end of the driveway, he started to feel less tense and turned toward Studemont.

"Hey Hammond!"

Seth let out a high-pitched shriek that probably sent every dog in the neighborhood into a frenzy. He was suddenly convinced that his father had known his plans all along, that he had somehow read Seth's mind and had only allowed his son enough rope with which to hang himself. Seth starting preparing a number of unlikely excuses and explanations, including trying to convince his father that he was sleepwalking.

But it wasn't his father that Seth found leaning against the waist-high brick wall that bordered the Stevenson's yard next door. It was Dirk, bent over with a hand planted on each knee, laughing so hard he seemed unable to catch his breath. His ever-present cigarette dangled from his lips, in danger of falling as the laughter continued.

Seth glanced around, expecting to see lights coming on in the surrounded houses, doors to open and curious neighbors to stumble out onto their porches to see what all the commotion was. His father was a fairly sound sleeper, but Seth's piercing scream was surely loud enough to have stirred coma patients from their slumber.

"Oh Hammond, that was priceless," Dirk said between hiccuping breaths. The laughter was tapering, but tears leaked from his eyes. "Man, you screamed like some chick from a horror movie, about to be impaled by a machete or something. And your face, I thought you were gonna have a heart-attack."

"Can we laugh at my humiliation later, like when we're a couple of blocks away from my house?"

"Sure thing." Dirk started down the sidewalk at a brisk pace, Seth trailing behind, constantly casting glances over his shoulder as if he expected his father to appear at any moment.

Only when they turned the corner by the post office did Seth start to relax. Dirk had said nothing since they'd started walking, had merely finished one cigarette and started another. "So," Seth said, "how come you were at my house? I thought I was supposed to meet you at the graveyard."

"I figured since you were new in town, you might have trouble finding it."

"Oh, that was awfully considerate of you."

Dirk cut his eyes at Seth and smirked. "It doesn't mean you're my girlfriend or nothing, just didn't want you to get lost. No big deal."

"Oh yeah, of course, no big deal," Seth said, wishing he sounded more suave instead of like the world's biggest spaz.

"I hear you and your old man are from Washington State."

"Yeah, Seattle."

"Why the hell did ya'll move all the way to this piss-ant town for?"

"It's a long, not particularly interesting story."

"I hear your ma dumped Hard-ass."

"Who told you that?" Seth said, stopping suddenly. He jaw clenched and his hands balled up into fists at his side.

Dirk turned and looked at Seth with his head cocked to one side, as if he were a scientist studying a newly discovered specimen. "It's just the word going around. One thing you'll learn fast about small town life, everybody knows everything about everybody. Is it true about your ma?"

Seth nodded and the two started walking again. "I don't really want to talk about it."

"I hear that. My pop ran out on us when I was six."

"Really?"

"Yep, him and some floozy from the Roughneck Roadhouse out on Highway 18 took off together."

"You ever hear from him?"

"Not a word since the day he left. Hell, he could be dead for all I know."

"Well, my Mom calls a couple times a week. I'm supposed to go spend Christmas vacation with her."

"You looking forward to it?"

"Not particularly. She's moved in with this twenty-two year old guy. He's only six years older than me, for Christ's sake."

"Doesn't sound like much fun."

"No, but I don't imagine I'd have much fun here with Dad, either."

"Stuck between a Slut and a Hard-ass."

Seth's first reaction was to get angry at the way Dirk was talking about his parents, but then he found himself laughing. It wasn't anything he hadn't thought about them himself. Dirk glanced over at him and started laughing as well. It was the first time Seth could remember laughing since he'd gotten to Paddington, and it felt good.

"Well, Hammond, here we are."

They had arrived at the corner of Glenavon and Studemont and were standing outside a rusty iron gate. A red brick wall enclosed several acres of what appeared to be an empty dirt lot. There were no streetlamps here, but there was a flickering light glowing somewhere on the other side of the gate, and Seth squinted through the iron bars and saw only darkness, a dead tree with skeletal branches devoid of leaves reaching up toward the sky, and a pole as tall as the tree with a sign at its apex. The sign read, *Ed Sacks Waste Paper Co. 410 Studemont.*

"What is this?" Seth asked. "I thought we were going to a graveyard."

"This is it, the Graveyard. Come on, the guys are probably already here."

The gate squeaked as Dirk pushed it open, and flakes of rust fell into his hair. Seth hesitated a moment before following the older boy through the opening. "You come here a lot?"

"Yeah. Not much else to do in this town, you know. They used to keep the gate padlocked, but after some of us broke the lock with a crowbar a couple of times, they finally gave up. Not like there's anything here to steal."

They walked past the sign and headed for the tree. There were two metal trash barrels underneath it, and in one of them a fire had been set, orange flames licking the air as black smoke chugged upward like a mushroom cloud. Three of Dirk's buddies were standing next to the fire, drinking beer from aluminum cans.

"Yo, Dirk!" called a black guy in camouflage pants and a neatly maintained Afro. "What took you so long?"

"Had to make a little detour. Guys, I want you to meet Hammond. Hammond, these are the guys. The brother over there is Terrell, the beanpole who's already so drunk he can barely stand is Kent, and you already know Ryan."

Terrell stepped forward, the fire casting dancing shadows across his dark-skinned face, and said, "Hey, ain't you the principal's kid?"

Seth nodded and crossed his arms over his chest, feeling slightly queasy and wondering why he'd come here in the first place.

"Holy Mother of Fuck!" Kent said loudly. He was tall, well over six feet, and must have weighed all of one hundred and twenty-five pounds, and just as Dirk had said, he seemed about three sheets to the wind. Hell, four or five sheets. "Hard-ass Hammond's kid, we're all gonna be in trouble now!"

"Keep it down," Dirk said, and there was authority in his voice. "Hammond's cool."

Ryan stepped over and slapped Kent on the back, nearly sending the inebriated boy toppling to the ground. "Yeah, he pulled Dirk's ass outta the fire at school today. Saved him from getting expelled."

"Shit, he didn't do you no favor then," Terrell said with a laugh. "If he'd *got* you expelled, now that'd be something to celebrate."

"We can't all be high school dropouts with a bright future in the fast food industry like you, man."

Terrell held up the middle finger of each hand, shooting Dirk the double bird, and everyone laughed. Even Seth.

"You guys ain't drunk all the beer yet, I hope," Dirk said.

Ryan flipped open the lid of a small red cooler, and Seth could see three silver cans floating in a couple inches of water, which he assumed had started the night as ice. "We managed to save you a few, but it wasn't easy keeping 'em away from Kent."

Kent, who had been staggering in a circle and humming the tune to *The Jeffersons*, came to attention at the sound of his name. "I got a thirst, man," he said, his words slurring together. "Gotta clench the thirst."

"I think you mean *quench* the thirst, shit-for-brains." Dirk snagged two of the beers from the cooler. "Want one, Hammond?"

Seth started to decline but then thought better of it. These guys were welcoming him into their fold; it would be impolite not to share a drink with them. Never mind the fact that he'd never had a sip of alcohol before in his life. First time for everything, as the old saying went.

Popping the tab, Seth tried to look nonchalant, as if he drank beer all the time. He took a tentative sip and had to force himself not to grimace. The taste was sour, but he forced it down and took another sip. Not that he knew firsthand, but he imagined it was a bit like drinking urine.

Apparently detecting the disgust Seth was trying to keep off his face, Dirk said, "I know, it doesn't taste as good when it's warm, but you take what you can get."

Seth smiled and took another sip.

Dirk closed the cooler and sat on top of it, taking a long swallow of his beer. "So where're the rest of the guys?"

Ryan sat on the ground, his back leaned against the trunk of the tree. "Ain't heard from Gerry, but Wes is out on a date with Paige."

"Oh man, Wes still trying to get some from that chick? What is this, their fourth date? About time he faced it, the bitch don't put out."

"Oh yeah she does," Terrell said, sticking his face dangerously close to the fire to light a cigarette off the flames. "She just likes dark meat, if you know what I mean."

"You kidding me?" Ryan said and let loose with his loon laugh. "You saying you fucked her?"

"Well, not exactly. Paige comes from a good Catholic family, so let's just say she participated in a little mouth-to-cock resuscitation."

Seth shifted from one foot to the other, nursing his warm beer. Graphic sex talk always made him uncomfortable, probably because he was still a virgin. He'd gotten to second base with Sheryl Arnold back in Seattle, but that was the extent of his experience with women. It had seemed like a big deal at the time, but compared to these guys, Seth was practically a eunuch.

While Dirk and his buddies continued to discuss the various talents of Paige and other girls they knew, Seth studied the lot. Not that there was much to see. Other than the tree under which they all stood, there was nothing but dirt and discarded beer cans, potato chip bags, and even condom wrappers. Something at the far end of the lot caught his attention. It was hard to make out with only the fire for light, but as his eyes adjusted, he realized that across the back wall someone had spray-painted the word GRAVEYARD. The letters were as tall as the wall itself and done in white paint.

"Hey, principal's kid," Kent said suddenly, weaving his way over to Seth. "Can you talk? I ain't heard you open your mouth since you got here."

Surely that couldn't be true, but Seth realized it was. He hadn't spoken a word since arriving at the lot. He stared around at the four other guys, who were all staring back at him now. He looked to Dirk for assistance, but he was just sitting there with a faint smile on his lips.

"I've just been waiting for someone to say something interesting, and it hasn't happened yet," Seth said, not sure where the words had come from.

Silence filled the lot for several seconds, and Seth started to wonder if his attempt at humor had been a mistake. Ryan was the first to laugh, his trademark giggle that was starting to grow on Seth, and the other three joined in soon after. Seth doubled up and ended up on his ass in the dirt, his own laughter tearing out of him like something alive and eager to escape.

"Okay," Terrell said with a grin, "then what do you wanna talk about?"

Seth, just wanting to get the conversation turned away from sex, asked the first thing that came to mind. "What exactly is this place?"

Dirk pointed up to the sign. "Used to be home to Ed Sacks Waste Paper, but that closed down about fourteen years ago. It was Paddington's only major industry, and the town's been dying a slow death ever since."

"They tore the place down in 2000," Ryan said. "Were supposedly gonna put up a strip mall or something, but it never happened."

"Who did the artwork on the back wall?"

Dirk glanced over at the graffiti and said softly, "That was our friend, Randall."

"Where's he?"

Nobody said anything for a moment, and Seth felt a tension in the air. Kent was the one to answer, and he sounded somber if not sober. "He died early last year."

"Oh, I'm sorry. I didn't realize."

"Don't worry about it," Dirk said, finishing off his beer, crushing the can, tossing it behind his back, and lighting up a cigarette. "Nobody's fault but his own. He overdosed on heroine."

"Randall was certainly a partier," Ryan said. "Just didn't know when to stop."

Dirk nodded. "You can say that again. After that, we all made a pact to stay off that shit. No drugs for us except the booze."

"And a little weed now and then," Terrell said.

Dirk smiled. "And a little weed now and then."

Seth took another drink of his beer and was surprised to find the can empty. Apparently he had grown accustomed to the taste, or else it had dulled his taste buds, because he had found it going down a lot easier after the first few sips. He felt a little lightheaded, but not in a bad way. Sort of like his head was floating a few feet above his body, a balloon tethered to his neck.

Dirk raised himself up just enough to open the cooler and snag the last beer. "Here you go, Hammond." He tossed the can and Seth actually managed to catch it. "Looks like it's time for Terrell to make another beer run."

"Shit man, why I always gotta be the one to go on the beer runs?"

"Because you're the only one of us who's twenty-one," Ryan said.

"Sucks being the oldest one in the group. You dickheads need to get your asses some fake IDs."

"I had one," Dirk said. "Got confiscated when I tried to use it to get in that titty bar over in Lincoln."

"Well, I'll be glad when you babies finally grow up so I ain't always gotta go for the beer."

Ryan stood up, wiping dirt off the seat of his pants. "Jesus, stop your bitching. The all-night Fast Fare is only a block and a half down Glenavon. I'll walk over with you."

"Me, too," Kent said then fell flat on his back. He mumbled, rolled over on his side, and began to snore.

Dirk checked his watch. "Made it almost to one o'clock before passing out. Think that's some kinda record."

They all chipped in a few bucks for the beer, all except for Kent who was curled up in the fetal position a few feet away. Terrell and Ryan headed off for the Fast Fare, Terrell still griping about having to always be the beer-getter.

Dirk and Seth sat in silence for a while, the only sound the crackling of the fire and the buzz saw grinding of Kent's snores. Finally Dirk looked Seth's way and said, "Having fun?"

"Yeah," Seth said and started giggling for no reason. Somehow his second beer was already half empty; he wasn't sure how that happened. "Thanks for inviting me. I never do stuff like this."

"Well, I always do stuff like this. Almost every night, the same thing. Drinking at the Graveyard. Smoking at the Graveyard. The same old guys, the same old routine."

Seth stopped giggling. The flames had died down, and Dirk was sitting in a deep pocket of shadow so Seth couldn't see his face, but there had been something melancholy about his tone. Seth wanted to say something, but he wasn't sure what.

"How you like Paddington so far?" Dirk asked.

"I think it's pretty much a shithole."

Dirk chuckled. "You ain't wrong about that. And the longer you stay here, the deeper you get sucked into the shit."

"Well, I can see why you're not on the Welcoming Committee."

"They should put me on the Welcoming Committee. I'd try to scare people away from this town, save them from the fate of getting stuck in this—as you so eloquently put it—shithole. I'd be doing a public service."

"You should bring that up at the next town meeting."

They fell back into silence, Seth finishing his beer and Dirk going through another cigarette. Kent muttered something in his sleep that sounded like, "Possum ate all my gravy." A car went by on Studemont, its headlights briefly lighting up the lot. Dirk blew a smoke ring into the air and said, "I really do appreciate you not ratting me out to your old man today."

"It's not that big a deal."

"Yeah, it is. I'm sure you got into a fair amount of trouble with Hard-ass."

"A little."

"You didn't have to do that, especially not for some asshole who'd given you nothing but grief since you started school. I don't know many would've done it."

"Well, my dad can be pretty unreasonable sometimes, and he just seemed to be taking a little too much pleasure in the prospect of kicking you out of school."

"You saved my ass, that's for damn sure. Now if I can just manage not to flunk out, I should be okay."

"Your classes tough?"

"They shouldn't be, it's the second time I've had 'em. If I fail again, that's it. No diploma for me. This is my last shot."

"You ever consider dropping out like Terrell?"

"Shit, of course I've thought about it, but it would break my ma's heart. Since Pop split when I was so young, she's really had to work her ass off to keep me and my younger sister up. She don't ask for much, she just wants to see me graduate. I've been such a troublemaker my whole life, I'd like to do this one thing to make her proud."

"And what about after you graduate?"

"My Uncle Art runs a used car lot, he says I can have a job as a salesman. I'll probably take him up on it, marry some nice little hometown gal, and die a slow death along with everyone else in this town."

"I don't get it. If you hate this town so much, why stay here?"

Dirk laughed, but this time there was no humor in the sound. "You say that as if I had some choice in the matter."

"You do. There's no law that says just because you grew up here you have to live here the rest of your life."

"You're the new kid on the block, Hammond, so you don't quite understand how things work yet. Nobody gets out of the Graveyard alive."

"What are you talking about? It's just some empty lot."

"More proof you just don't get it. This lot isn't the Graveyard; this *town* is the Graveyard. Paddington. It's like stepping in quicksand, it just keeps pulling you under and there's no escaping it."

Seth wasn't sure how to respond to such despondency. After rejecting various responses, he finally said, rather lamely, "What about college?"

"Yeah, maybe I'll get a scholarship to Harvard or Yale. I ain't the college type, Hammond. You barely know me, but I'm sure you figured that much out already."

"Okay, so maybe you don't go to college, but you could get a job in another city. Your Uncle Art's isn't the only car dealership in the world."

"It's a nice little dream, but that's all it is. I already got my tombstone picked out and everything. My pop rode that floozy right out of Paddington, leaving his son here to be buried in his place."

Seth opened his mouth to spout some horrible cliché—it's always darkest before the dawn, every cloud has a silver lining, tomorrow's another day—but was saved the embarrassment when the gate squeaked open and Terrell and Ryan came walking across the lot, each carrying a six pack.

"Never fear," Terrell said, "here comes the beer."

***

It was almost six a.m., and the sun was peeking over the horizon. The fire had died out several hours ago, leaving the air tasting like ashes. Seth and Dirk were the only two left in the Graveyard. Just past four, Kent had awoken and begun throwing up in the second trash barrel. Terrell and Ryan had agreed to walk him home, and they'd left with Kent propped up between them. Seth and Dirk reclined under the tree, drinking beers and chatting about school, about their folks. When they ran out of things to say, they settled into a comfortable silence without the pressure to fill it with words. Seth stopped after four and a half beers; watching Kent upchuck everything short of his intestines had gone a long way toward tempering his desire to drink.

As the sun lightened the sky to a soft pink, Seth glanced at his watch. "Damn man, I need to get back home."

"What's that?" Dirk said, swiveling his head unsteadily toward Seth. Dirk had not slowed his drinking after Kent had gotten sick, and he was fairly well intoxicated by this point.

"I said I need to get home."

"Come on man, it's early," Dirk said, and then laughed uproariously as his own slight joke.

Seth stood and stretched until his back popped. "I know, but my dad gets up at seven a.m. on the weekends."

"You gotta get up early in the morning to be a Hard-ass, I guess."

Seth gave a polite laugh, then shifted uncertainly. "Well, I had a good time. I'm glad you let me tag along."

"My pleasure," Dirk said with a grand wave of his hands. "You alright to find your way back to your house?"

"Yeah, I think I can manage without getting lost. What do you guys have going on tonight?"

"Same shit, different day."

Stuffing his hands in his pockets, Seth rocked on the balls of his feet and chewed on his lower lip. "Maybe I can hang out with you guys here tonight?"

"No."

Dirk's answer was so unexpected that at first it didn't register with Seth. He blinked, stammered for a second, then said, "What?"

"No, you can't hang out with us tonight. You're not invited."

"Oh, I thought..." *we were friends* was how Seth intended to finish his statement but couldn't get the words out.

Dirk leaned forward, pulling his knees up to his chest. "Look Hammond, I was just paying back a favor you did me by inviting you here tonight; now we're even."

Seth felt like crying, which made him angry at himself. He had dared think maybe he'd finally made a friend for the first time since moving to Paddington, and it turned out Dirk was just repaying a debt, seeing Seth as nothing more than an obligation. "Well, I didn't mean to be a nuisance or anything."

Dirk looked Seth in the eye, the rising sun blazing behind his head making him look like he had hair of fire, and he suddenly seemed less drunk than he had only a moment before. "Look Hammond, I'm gonna be straight with you. I said no one gets out of the Graveyard alive, but that wasn't entirely true. Sometimes certain people break free, and you're one of those people. I can just tell. You don't belong in the Graveyard."

"Yeah, but that doesn't mean—"

"You can't hang with corpses without becoming one. That's a fact."

Seth knew he should leave, but he couldn't make his feet move. He just kept staring at Dirk until the older boy finally leaned back against the tree trunk and closed his eyes. Seth wanted to say something, but there was nothing more to be said. Finally he turned and made his way back across the dirt lot. Terrell, Kent, and Ryan had left the gate open, and Seth paused just before going through it.

He glanced back toward the tree. The sun was erupting over the back wall, and the last thing Seth saw before leaving the lot was Dirk raising his hand in a silent wave as the dawn light silhouetted his form against the graffiti of a dead boy. Then Seth turned and left the Graveyard.

www.ingramcontent.com/pod-product-compliance
Lightning Source LLC
Chambersburg PA
CBHW061155170626
46809CB00003B/1101